WALK

a thriller

VICTOR METHOS

Copyright 2012 Victor Methos
Kindle & Print Edition
License Statement

This book is licensed for your personal enjoyment only. This book may not be re-sold or given away to other people. If you would like to share this book with another person, please purchase an additional copy for each recipient. If you're reading this book and did not purchase it, or it was not purchased for your use only, then please return to Amazon.com and purchase your own copy. Please note that this is a work of fiction. Any similarity to persons, living or dead, is purely coincidental. All events in this work are purely from the imagination of the author and are not intended to signify, represent, or reenact any event in actual fact.

Hell is empty, and all the devils are here.

-William Shakespeare

1

Detective Jonathan Stanton pulled out his sidearm and fell into the Weaver stance, the muzzle a few feet from Darrell Putnam's forehead. The wind, thirty-four floors up on the roof of One American Plaza, screamed in his ears and muffled the rest of the world.

"Don't do it, Darrell," he shouted. "There's no need for this."

Putnam yelled something. The sentence was long, but Stanton couldn't decipher much of it. The one thing he was able to make out toward the end was, "I didn't do it."

"If you didn't do it, you'll walk. But I need you to come back with me. I gotta talk to you and check out what you tell me. You know the routine, Darrell. We've been through this before. If you tell me the truth, I can help you out."

Putnam nodded, looking down at the rubber flooring. The roof was clean and uncluttered, and he ran his foot in a circle on the surface. He looked up and smiled, then he turned and leapt off the edge.

Stanton ran to grab him, but it was too late. He leaned over the side and watched the man plummet toward the ground. He wanted to look away. After a decade in Homicide, he had so many images of bloody, torn bodies lingering in his mind. Screams and pleas whispered to him at night in the calm moments before sleep. He didn't want to add this one as well.

But in the end, he watched Putnam slam into a van turning at the intersection, collapsing the roof and exploding the tires.

Stanton turned away. For just a moment, he looked up to the sun and let it warm his face. He closed his eyes and pretended he was on the beach, listening to the surf hit the shore and feeling it wash over his feet in cool waves.

The cell phone in his pocket vibrated. He turned it off and headed for the stairs.

By the time Stanton got to the first floor, the Channel 8 news van was already there. A stylist was applying makeup to an attractive blonde while the cameraman and sound guy set up. Crowds had gathered, and officers were in the street, directing traffic.

Several paramedics were helping a man sitting in the back of an ambulance. Stanton assumed this was the driver of the vehicle hit by the falling man. He looked shaken, and he had suffered cuts over his face and arms from the glass shattering in every one of his windows, but he was alive.

Stanton peeked into the van just as someone from the county medical examiner's office came to a stop across the street. Several more cruisers pulled up, followed by an unmarked Dodge Charger driven by Detective Daniel Childs.

Childs stepped out of the car, his arms bulging underneath the tight polyester shirt he preferred to wear instead of the traditional button-down and suit coat. His shining badge dangled from a chain around his neck, and his .45 Smith & Wesson was tucked into a sleek black holster on his hip. Childs was the first African American detective accepted into the San Diego County Sex Crimes Strike Force.

"What happened?" he asked, stopping next to Stanton.

"He jumped."

"From One American? No shit? I didn't think he had the balls." He stepped closer, his face contorting in disgust as he saw that bloody splotches of Putnam's brain matter covered the interior of the van. "Mess with little kids and this is where you belong." He slapped Jon's shoulder. "Good work."

Stanton didn't move. Unblinking, he stared at the remains, observing the flow of black blood rolling from the van and pooling on the pavement.

"Jon, snap out of it, man. This is a good thing."

"The last thing he said is that he didn't do it."

"So what? Every piece of shit we deal with says he didn't do it."

"He knew he was going to die, and he still said he didn't do it."

"So what? You're overthinking this, man. That's what you get when you spend too many years in college. Come on, let's let the rookies clean this up. Give your statement and your firearm over and come grab a drink with me at Coochies."

Stanton bit the inside of his cheek then ran his tongue over the indentation, feeling the soft membranes. He pulled out his firearm and handed it to Childs to hold as he took out the second revolver he carried in a holster against the small of his back.

"What's that for?"

"Life's unpredictable. Always carry a backup, Danny." He walked over to some of the uniforms and gave a summary of what had happened, along with his weapons, and turned back to Childs, who was still looking into the van. "All right. You drive."

2

Coochies stank like cigarette smoke and vomit, but most bars in San Diego couldn't match the appeal of its proximity to the water on Ocean Beach. When the doors and windows were open, the salty breeze washed over the patrons, leaving the taste of sea salt on their tongues. A lot of cops visited the bar because it hadn't developed a reputation as a cop bar. Once that reputation set in, the police officers who went there to relax could expect all the cop groupies to come out of the woodwork, trying to fit in, tell war stories, and catch the latest gossip about the precincts.

A country song played over the speakers, and for now, the bar was filled only with surfers calling it a day with a final drink. Most of the patrons were still in their bathing suits. Stanton and Childs sat in a booth in the corner.

A young waitress waved at them then grabbed a Heineken and a bottle of Diet Coke before coming over. "Hey, guys."

"Hey," Stanton said. "How are ya, Eve?"

"Doing good. Busy, busy. How are my boys?"

"Not bad. Not great, but not bad."

Childs blew through his teeth dismissively. "He's too down. We had a great resolution to something we'd been working on for months. In fact, I think, Johnny boy, you should have a real man's drink. Mormon church won't kill you if you have one shot of tequila."

"Oh, quit giving him shit, Danny. Drink your beer and play nice."

"You know I always do. So Evie, when you comin' out with me?"

"Told you, baby, I don't date cops. Too much drama."

"Pssh, you just scared. When you had enough of them surfer boys and want a man, you come see me."

She placed her hand on his shoulder. "I'm not sure you'd know what to do with me if you got me, baby."

Childs watched her walk away and shook his head as he took a long gulp of his beer. "She doesn't know how crazy she makes me."

"Have you asked her out?"

"Asked her out? What is this, 1953? Should we go and get a soda and catch a drive-in?"

"Sounds good to me."

He chuckled. "You from a different time, man. This ain't your decade."

Stanton smiled as he spun the glass of dark soda. He let the ice clink in the glass then took out one of the cubes and sucked on it.

"That shit today is sticking with you, huh?"

"I don't know what it is. You're right; everyone says they didn't do it. But when he said it, I was looking him in the eyes and… if you read the research on death penalty cases, offenders usually apologize and express remorse for their actions, or they blame the victim, trying to hurt the survivors with their last words. I just never saw anyone maintain their innocence when they knew they were about to die."

"Man, come on. We got all the evidence we needed. Judge signed off on the warrant, we got his own mama talking about what a sick shit he was, and he was on the sex offender registry with two priors. What else you want? An email saying, 'Hey, I love kiddies. Come get me'? That ain't gonna happen."

"I know," Stanton said, shaking his head as if pushing the thoughts out of his mind. "I know. It's stupid. We got our guy."

"That's damn right, we got our guy." He held up his beer and tapped it against Stanton's glass. "To getting our guy and watching him throw his ass off the tallest building in the city."

3

He could see the heat waves coming off the pavement that surrounded the dry soccer field. The girls wore yellow-and-black uniforms, like bumblebees. Grinning, he leaned back in his seat and put his feet up on the dashboard. The Volkswagen Beetle was too small. He was muscular and had added thirty pounds over the last year; he would need a bigger car as soon as he could afford it, but all his money seemed to go toward training and food these days.

He rolled up his window and turned on the air conditioning, but the air that came out of the vents was nearly as warm as the air outside, so he turned it off and rolled the window back down. Having the window down was better anyway. The smell of the recently cut grass reminded him of the fields his uncle had taken him to as a child to watch football games.

What was his name? He couldn't remember, and that bothered him for a moment, until he saw her.

He watched her from the second she stepped out of her mother's Jeep, her gym bag slung over her shoulder, and his eyes followed her as she walked to the field. She threw her bag down near the others and ran to her coach and the rest of her team. Most of the parents didn't stay, and hers was no exception. The Jeep turned and pulled out of the junior high school parking lot.

He scanned the rows of bags along the field and saw hers. It was black with red handles, and a sticker of some Disney singer was stuck to the side. His fingers itched and he rubbed them together, running his tongue over his teeth and feeling the dryness of his mouth. He opened the door and stepped outside.

This is insanity. He was wearing shorts and a tank top and had his natural color hair. The tattoos of characters from *Alice in Wonderland* he had sleeved on his arms were easily identifiable.

This is insanity.

But he still couldn't stop himself.

He sauntered forward, glancing around. Maybe twenty feet stood between him and the bag, and he stopped as the coach yelled something out. As the players hustled into groups and began doing wind sprints, he moved toward the bag again. He was on the grass now.

Going out onto the field with his face exposed could ruin everything, but the excitement tingled his belly and quickened his breath. Emotion was something he rarely felt. Adrenaline coursed through him, and for a brief moment, he felt invincible.

He looked at the bag; the zipper was open six or seven inches. Inside were the clothes she planned to change into after showering. She showered in the school locker room with the rest of the team because several of the girls were also in madrigals and had singing practice for forty-five minutes after soccer.

He reached for her jeans. The thought of touching her clothing excited him, and he held his breath as sweat rolled down his forehead.

"Can I help you?"

He looked up and saw a woman standing over him with her arms folded. She was eyeing his tattoos, and she had already taken out her cell phone.

"Oh, hi. Um, no, I don't think so. I'm Lexi's uncle. She's missing madrigals today, and her mom just asked me to hang out until she's done." He stood and held out his hand. "Jack Woods."

She stared at his hand then cautiously put hers out and shook it. As soon as was practicable, she pulled away and wiped her palm on her jeans.

"Helluva team," he said. "I think Coach Dykes is gonna take 'em all the way. Which one's yours?"

The look on the woman's face softened, and she looked out over the field at a brunette girl near the goalpost. "Macey's my oldest."

"Oh, she's great. That goal she scored last week against Bennion was one of the best ones I'd seen all season."

"Oh, you saw that game? Yeah, that was good. She told us later she didn't think she was gonna make it, but they were down by one, so she said a Hail Mary and went for it."

He smiled as the woman continued to talk, but his attention wasn't on her. He glanced over at the field, where Lexi was running from one goal post to the next. He looked down at her bag.

Such a shame.

"You know what," he said, "I got something you might like. I promised Lexi I wouldn't do this 'cause it embarrasses her, but it's some photos of her when she was two. She'd dress up in a soccer uniform and kick a ball around her mom's house."

"Oh, I would love to see those."

"I'll grab 'em. Be right back."

The car was as hot as ever when he climbed in. The woman was turned around, clapping for her daughter who had finished the sprints before everyone else. He started his car and sped out of the parking lot.

He'd taken an unprecedented risk, and he'd crapped out. The woman would certainly remember him and his car. He should've chosen one of the other girls as his "niece," but he'd been caught off guard.

I'm never caught off guard. This was a disaster.

But it could've been much worse.

He would have to let Lexi go. He was amused thinking she would never know how close she'd come to sharing time with him; but the woman would surely remember him.

Then again, she might not.

4

Stanton drove Childs's car to his house then called a cab. Childs didn't just drink to have a good time, to lubricate conversation, or to relieve stress. He drank to get obliterated. Sometimes he got so drunk that he would strike out at Stanton, unable to recognize him, and blurt out drunken slurs before passing out at the bar, on the dance floor, or at someone's house during a poker game. Stanton wanted to speak with him about the issue, but Childs knew Stanton held a PhD in psychology and refused to talk about personal matters around him.

When Stanton climbed in, the cabbie was soft spoken, and the interior smelled like sweet yogurt and hummus.

"Where you from?" Stanton asked after a brief conversation about the wonderful smell.

"Palestine."

"I've always wanted to go to the Middle East, but things keep coming up. I have two sons, and I just have a hard time leaving them for long."

"There is nothing better, though, than going home to family."

"That's true. But they live with their mother."

"Divorced?"

"Yeah."

"It is strange here, everybody divorce. People married twenty, thirty years, and they divorce. In Palestine, when you promise to be married, you married. No divorce."

"We expect to be happy here. Most people in other countries don't expect that."

When they arrived at Stanton's place, he paid and thanked the cabbie for the ride.

His sparsely decorated apartment held little more than furniture, clothes, toiletries, a television, and some art deco posters on the walls. Stanton threw his keys on the table and walked out on the balcony.

His eleventh-floor apartment looked out over the busy intersection below. Beyond it, the choppy Pacific Ocean appeared dark blue, like melted sapphire. The apartment was really a condo that belonged to an old man who had used it as a winter home. He lived in New Hampshire and wanted to rent to someone single. But when he'd found out Stanton was a cop, he dropped his price by fifteen percent and faxed over the lease right away, assuming a cop would take good care of the place.

Stanton watched the water a long time then glanced at the pavement eleven floors down. It was swarming with people who seemed not to notice each other. He went to the second bedroom, which he had turned into an office.

Though investigations were paperless now and files were uploaded onto a shared database, Stanton made hard copies of all his files. There was just something about holding paper in his hands that a computer screen could never match. Paper was personal. When reading reports of monsters who had invaded people's lives, he felt at times like an intruder, and somehow the soft paper between his fingers assured him that he had permission.

Thick files took up most of the shelf in his closet, all representing stolen lives. He pulled out the file marked "Darrell Putnam."

Putnam had never had a chance at life. The parole board's ordered psychological evaluation was twenty-three pages long. Twenty-three pages explained an entire life.

At the age of ten, he had been molested by a priest at his local parish. The abuse had continued for over three years, until he developed such bad anxiety and depression that he was sent to the school counselor, where he opened up about what had occurred. The counselor had notified the police. When they arrived at the church offices to interview the priest, he pulled a gun out of a drawer and placed it between his lips before pulling the trigger.

Putnam had been disruptive in school but not violent. He didn't get his first criminal charge—driving while intoxicated—until he was nineteen. At twenty-three, he was arrested for sexually abusing his neighbor's ten-year-old son.

He was released from prison after serving six years, and within three months, he had abused another boy in a shopping mall bathroom stall. After serving fourteen years, he voluntarily underwent chemical castration and was paroled early. He had been out for six years without incident when he'd become a suspect in Stanton's investigation.

The doorbell rang, startling him out of his thoughts. He closed the file and carried it out of the bedroom with him, placing it on the kitchen counter before answering the door.

Sandra Porter stood there, leaning one arm against the frame, her badge clipped to her belt. She held a six-pack of Diet Coke in her other hand.

"Thought you could use some company after today."

"I could."

She walked in and sat on the couch before picking up the Rubik's cube on the coffee table. "You couldn't have stopped him if he really wanted to die. You should just be grateful he didn't want suicide by cop."

"Maybe."

"What's wrong?"

"Nothing."

"Don't give me that nothing, Jon. We've been dating for six months, and every little secret about you still needs to be dragged out like rotting teeth. What's going on?"

"He did something strange before he jumped that hasn't been sitting right with me."

"What?"

"He told me he's innocent."

"Everyone says that."

"I know. It sounds crazy, and I have no reason to back it up, but I think he might've been telling the truth."

"Well, you got two options: You can choose not to believe him and close the case with a win and some slaps on the back. I heard Chief Rodriguez is thinking about giving you some sort of commendation for it."

"What's the other option?"

"You can believe him, which means you still got one vile prick out there killing children."

5

Gary R. Coop sat at his desk inside the Emerald Plaza building in downtown San Diego. His office was near the top floor; it had white carpets with deep cherry wood paneling and furniture to match. The couches and chairs were imported leather, and the secretaries and paralegals at his law firm were the most beautiful he could find. He had always believed employees could be trained to do a good job, but someone either had beauty or didn't.

He was reading through a document when he set it down on the desk and leaned back, absently playing with his Rolex Yacht-Master. He caught a glimpse of its reflection in the window and grinned. Less than twenty years ago, the owners hadn't wanted to rent office space to him in this building because he was black. Now his law firm owned two entire floors.

Coop pressed a button on his phone.

"Yeah, boss?"

"Jeremy, come in here, will you please?"

A young man of twenty-eight stepped into the office and sat down across from him. Jeremy was wearing a pinstripe Armani suit, not unlike the one Coop was wearing. "What's up?"

"Take a look at this." He slid the document across the desk. "It's that pedophile who jumped off the roof over at the American."

He flipped through the pages quietly for a few minutes.

"What about it?" he finally said.

"You don't see anything there?"

Jeremy shook his head. "Guy jumped. Cop didn't throw him

off."

"No, but he may as well have. He had a gun pointed at his head. Look at the profile on the detective. History of depression and even a stay in a psychiatric ward. He quit the force for a long time and came back because Michael Harlow asked him to."

"Holy shit. That's where I know his name from. He's the cop that testified against Harlow."

"Biggest police corruption scandal in the city's history, Jeremy. I would've given my left nut to have defended Harlow. Thing was on the news damn near every night."

"I know what you're thinking, boss, but I don't think that's going to work with this."

"Why not?"

"The guy was a pedophile. What jury is gonna feel sorry enough for him to take taxpayer money and give it to us cause he jumped off a building?"

Coop smiled. "You're still young and don't realize what juries are, Jeremy. They're emotional animals. They'll reach a conclusion during opening statements based on how everyone looks and then find any reason they can during the trial to justify that stance. We don't have to win the whole trial. We just gotta win the first few hours."

"If you say it's a good case, it's a good case. I'm on board."

"Find out the next of kin on the pedophile and get me their number. And this is the first and last time we call him 'the pedophile.' Even just between us. His name's Mr. Putnam. Send out an email to everyone saying that, too."

"You got it."

As Jeremy left, Coop put his feet up on the desk and stared out the window at the open blue sky. Jeremy was too inexperienced to realize what they had: a cop with mental illness and a victim who'd flown off a building with no other witnesses around. Even if Mr. Putnam was a pedophile, all Coop needed was a handful of jurors, maybe two or three, who hated cops. They would do his work for him and convince the rest that even pedophiles had rights that shouldn't be violated.

Coop couldn't help but smile; he had been waiting a long time for a case like this.

6

On Monday morning, Stanton arrived at the SDPD Northern Division precinct and headed to his office near the back of the building. It was cramped and filled with too many files, but it was away from the commotion at the front of the building, where the drunks, wife-beaters, and gangsters were hauled in and locked into the holding tank.

The entire back section had been devoted to the Sex Crimes Strike Force, the brainchild of the new chief of police, Antonio "Bulldog" Rodriguez. Bulldog had earned a reputation for being aggressive on sex cases long before he'd been made chief. He thought they were special. As head of the sex crimes unit in the Central Division, Bulldog had started the briefings with a prayer, asking the Lord for strength to catch Satan's demons loose on the earth. Stanton had served briefly under him before being transferred to Northern, and he remembered Bulldog telling him once that the sex crimes detectives were God's chosen people. Even more than Homicide or Missing Persons, they were responsible for punishing the monsters who preyed on the helpless.

When Bulldog was made chief after Harlow's arrest, within seventy-two hours, the San Diego Police Department had a new sex crimes unit: the strike force. It consisted of twelve detectives, more than all the other strike forces in the department. Bulldog had hired a PR firm on the government dime to convince the public they needed the additional detectives he wanted to hire. The PR firm had played up a recent case of a young girl kidnapped and sexually assaulted as she walked home from school. Two men had assaulted her right there on the sidewalk, and at least half a dozen people had driven by without taking any action. Finally, a father in a minivan called the police.

The firm stirred up enough outrage that the city and county could have funded another twelve detectives had Bulldog asked for it. But his demands were modest: transfer five more sex crimes detectives from around the county to bring his team to twelve, replace those detectives with promotions from within, and replace the promotions with new hires. He got his five within two months.

Sitting down at his desk, Stanton checked his calendar. He had a unit meeting in ten minutes. He turned to a filing cabinet and pulled out three red file folders. Red files involved children.

The first one was a nine-year-old girl named Yvette Reynolds. The second, a ten-year-old named Sarah Henroid. The third and most recent case was another ten-year-old named Beth Szleky. All three had disappeared and were never found.

Technically, these cases belonged to Missing Persons or Child Abuse, but those units consisted of only a handful of detectives working seventy to ninety cases. They were overwhelmed and underfunded. Rodriguez had spent all he could setting up his new strike force, and instead of cutting back from other areas to fund MP, he began assigning cases from MP to the strike force. Missing children were all assumed to be sex crimes cases, anyway.

Though they went to different schools, the three girls lived within five miles of each other. Darrell Putnam lived right in the center, in between Yvette and Beth, a mile and a half from Sarah.

"Jon," Childs said, poking his head in, "meeting, nerdalinger. Let's go."

He closed the files and stood up to follow Childs out.

"What were you lookin' at?" Childs asked as they walked down the hallway.

"Putnam's cases."

"Still thinkin' about that?"

Stanton knew that Childs was thinking about it, too. Downplaying it and treating it as if it were no big deal was his coping mechanism, and Stanton wasn't going to take that away from him.

"It just isn't sitting right."

"Just 'cause he said so?"

"No, if that's all it was, I wouldn't have thought twice about it. I had doubts the entire time we were after him. Putnam never left his house. Surveillance reports show that he stayed locked up in there for weeks at a time, sometimes months. When would he have a chance to pick up three girls?"

"We weren't on him twenty-four-seven. Don't underestimate these shitbags."

"It wasn't just going out and getting them. He would've needed to stalk them and learn their routines, learn things about them. There was no way he could've learned about a ten-year-old girl's routine by sneaking out at midnight for a few hours."

"Well, why didn't you say anything before?"

That, Stanton knew, was the pertinent question. He'd engaged in the chase as much as anyone and didn't remember a single time he'd gone to his CO and said he was having doubts that Putnam was their guy.

They walked into the conference room and took seats. Sergeant Walters stood at the head of the table, his muscles bulging under his shirt. He was the second biggest guy in the room, next to Childs, and Stanton could tell Walters felt inadequate around the muscular detective.

"All right, ladies and gentlemen, let's chat." He opened a file and scanned it. "First off, there's a new policy in place regarding OT. All requests for OT must now be approved by Assistant Chief Ho. I know, I know, but you guys submitted over a hundred combined hours of OT last month. That's unacceptable. We need to stick to our budget, or they're gonna cut us back, so let's all make sure the overtime's in good order. Best way to do that is to run it by me or Detective Childs before sending in an approval sheet.

"Next we got Stanton and his flying chi-mo. Good job, Detective Stanton, for closing the Sandman cases."

A few cheers went up in the room, and Childs clapped. The unit had nicknamed Putnam the Sandman because all the girls had been kidnapped from their bedrooms during the night.

"Cleared it with the chief, Jon. There's not going to be any administrative leave. IAD already looked at it and determined it doesn't qualify as an officer-involved shooting since the prick jumped off himself, so you're good to go. Okay, next item of business..."

Childs leaned over to Stanton and whispered, "IAD already cleared you? Since when does that happen so fast?"

"Since never."

"That's what I'm saying. What you think's going on?"

"I have no idea."

7

Stanton stopped at police headquarters on his way home. The building made him uncomfortable, and he sat in his car for a moment to orient himself. He glanced at the three red files on the passenger seat then stepped out. When he went inside, he was struck by how little of it he remembered, even though he had worked in the building for a significant amount of time.

He rode the elevators to the fifth floor, and a chill went down his back when he stepped off. He turned down the hallway to the secured door that had led to the Cold Case Unit. He waited for a uniform to input the code for him before he walked in.

He thought the floor looked about the same as it had before. Several plush offices with glass desks and a large conference room with a flat screen were up at the front. On the farthest wall from him was a giant map of the world. Bold lettering across the top said: *Where in the World is Eli Sherman*. Pushpins marked places the former detective had been sighted after his escape from the hospital following a feigned suicide attempt. The newest one was Sao Paulo, Brazil.

Stanton remembered the night he had discovered Sherman was responsible for the deaths of at least two women, and possibly as many as twelve, and he recalled the pain as two slugs from Sherman's gun entered his body and flung him over the stairwell in his home.

"Jon?"

He turned to see Assistant Chief Chin Ho standing behind him, a smile on his face.

"How are ya, Chin?"

"Doing well. How are you holding up?"

"Doing okay."

"Were you told that IAD cleared you?"

"Yeah, actually, that's what I wanted to talk to you about."

"Sure," he said, folding his arms, "what about it?"

"I've never heard of a clearance this quickly after the death of a suspect. They didn't even interview me."

"They had your statements. I talked to them personally, and they said everything looked fine. Even sent forensics up to the roof, and everything appeared like you said it did."

Stanton noticed Ho's body swaying slightly. It lasted only for a few seconds, then Ho realized he was doing it and stopped, but the small motion was enough to give him away. He was hiding something. People tended to fidget or shift weight from foot to foot, causing a swaying motion, while being less than truthful.

"As long as everything's on the up-and-up."

"Jon," he said, slapping his shoulder, "Harlow's locked up. That day and age is over with. You need to relax. Look, I got a dinner date, but call me anytime. All right?"

"All right."

As Ho left, Stanton stood still in the office a long time. Before leaving, he turned to the board and stared at the pushpin in Sao Paulo.

Stanton left the parking lot and headed for the freeway entrance. The daylight was fading, and the clock on his dash said 6:27 p.m. He pulled over to the side of the road and watched the cars pass him. The old shack across the street housed a run-down, empty soda shop. A For Lease sign was up in one of the broken windows.

When he was a kid, soda shops were dying out, relics from an age that existed only in memories. People had a tendency to elevate the past while letting the present degrade, and Stanton remembered his father talking about the wholesome nature of soda shops and how their decline was a blow to American culture, even though he had rarely gone to them as a child.

Stanton looked at the files sitting next to him and picked up the one marked YR. The victim's home was only twenty minutes away. He flipped his car around and headed south.

8

The house was an old white rambler with a yellowed lawn and a 1980s Cadillac out front. The recently waxed car gleamed in the fading sunlight, and a Mothers Against Drunk Driving sticker graced the back window.

Stanton rang the doorbell once then waited a long time before someone answered.

A woman in her fifties opened the door, wiping her hands with a dishcloth. "Detective Stanton?"

Stanton instantly saw the look of horror in her eyes. She had been hanging on for so long to the hope that Yvette was still alive somewhere that she had convinced herself that the girl's death was impossible.

"I don't have any news, Shawna," he quickly said. "I just wanted to check in and see how you're doing."

"I'm getting along. Please, come in."

Plants and a few pieces of religious art decorated the interior of the house. The Virgin Mary hung above the fireplace and a candle burned beneath the painting. He sat on the sofa, and Shawna Reynolds sat next to him.

"Would you like anything?" she asked.

"I'm fine, thank you. How is everything?"

"It's quiet. Sometimes I turn on the television just to have some noise. Philip works all day, so I'm by myself. My sister comes over a lot now. I have two nieces and…" She looked down at the couch.

"It's okay, Shawna."

"I'm sorry. I just can't think about anything else. It's been almost fourteen months now, and I can't think of anything else. I just see her. Living on the streets or locked up in some house. I see her in a ditch in my dreams, and she's crying out to me." She reached for a tissue from a nearly empty box on the coffee table.

"I'm sorry to bring all this up. I shouldn't have come."

"No," she said, wiping her eyes. "No, I'm so glad you did. It helps me to see you. To know someone's still looking for my Yvette." She leaned her head back, took a deep breath, and closed her eyes. She whispered something to herself that Stanton couldn't make out.

He wondered why she hadn't asked about Putnam, then he realized the reason. "You haven't seen me in the news, have you?"

"No. I rarely watch television. What were you in the news for?"

"Shawna, the man that we think, or we thought, was responsible for kidnapping Yvette—his name was Darrell Putnam—he died. He flung himself off of a building trying to get away from me."

She didn't respond, but he noticed she had stopped breathing.

"I'm sorry. I should have called you. I figured you'd see it on the news and call me."

"Did he say... did he say anything about her?"

"No. We searched his house and didn't find anything, either. Everyone believed he was responsible for Yvette and two other girls, but I'm not sure now. I need to go through this all again and see what we missed."

"So you're saying you think the man that took her is still alive?"

"Yes."

"What do you need?"

"There's a connection between the three girls. We thought it was Putnam, but there's something else. Something we missed. I need to go through Yvette's things again."

"Her room hasn't been touched. I don't let anyone in there,

and Philip stays away from it."

"Is there anything you have of hers or anything else you can think of that we haven't already gone over? Friends you haven't told me about, teachers or doctors or any other adults she'd had contact with that we haven't spoken to? Anything like that?"

"Not that I can think of."

He nodded and glanced to a photo of Yvette up on the mantel. "I'd like to go through her room, with your permission."

"Of course. You know where it is."

Stanton went to the stairs leading to the basement. He built up an image of the room in his mind. He remembered the bed next to the door, a dresser drawer near the closet, and posters of Justin Bieber and Miley Cyrus on the walls. The room had smelled faintly of Yvette's bodywash—something fruity, something a child would pick thinking it made them seem older.

He saw her door at the bottom of the stairwell. Her name was spelled out in little block lettering. When he opened the door, it creaked, and he pushed it all the way against the wall and waited a few moments before going in.

The room hadn't been changed in the slightest. He went to the center and looked around. On the dresser, children's jewelry lay next to Yvette's softball trophies. A photo of her in a uniform, holding a small bat, was leaned against the wall on top of the dresser. Converse sneakers, the laces adorned with sparkly stickers, were sticking out from under the bed.

Stanton opened the closet and saw her clothing. The closet held nothing he hadn't seen before. Everything in the room had been catalogued by him or Forensics. But he wasn't there for more physical evidence. Childs had once told him, uncomfortably but truthfully, that he was like a hound, and hounds couldn't chase without a scent. He noticed that the aroma of bodywash was gone, replaced by the scent of dust and stale air in a room without ventilation.

He left and shut the door behind him.

9

It was dark by the time Stanton pulled into his parking stall in the underground lot, which was far nicer than anything a cop could afford. He wondered how much of a discount the condo owner had really given him on the rent.

He took the elevator to the lobby, where he waved at the security guard who sat in a booth by a second set of elevators that led to the condo units. The interior of the elevators consisted of mirrors, and he caught a glimpse of himself as he pressed the button for the eleventh floor. The door jarred back open as a young woman in a skirt and high heels ran through at the last second. She smiled and turned around, staring up at the numbers above the door before pressing the button for the sixth floor. Another man got on and smiled at her. He stood behind her and Stanton could see him staring at her backside. The woman stepped off on the sixth floor, and the other man's eyes followed her until the doors closed.

"I could hit that all night." He looked at Stanton, who didn't respond. The man got off on the tenth floor and glanced back at him once before heading into his condo.

Stanton got off on his floor and checked his mailbox next to the vending machines. He'd received a letter reminding him that his student loan payment was due, and he looked at the projected payoff date on the back of the letter: May 5, 2025. Though his PhD had been paid for by a tuition waiver, he was still paying on the loans for his undergraduate and master's degrees.

The apartment was warm, and he turned on the air conditioner before changing into shorts and going out onto his balcony. Two small bonfires burned on the beach, signaling the night surfers to come down. Stanton got his board off the balcony and threw on sandals before heading out.

This section of beach near Ocean Park was filled with tourists and families during the day, but in the evenings and at night, the hardcore surfers came out.

Newport Avenue, the primary business district of Ocean Beach, wasn't far, but independent stores filled it; the community had not allowed chain stores to open in their neighborhood. So the locals knew to throw the tourists out when the sun began going down; night belonged to the people who lived here.

As Stanton walked down the beach, several other surfers heading down shouted hellos or *alohas*. He was known as an "ace," a surfer who preferred to be in a solitary state of mind and connect with the ocean without distractions.

Ted came up to him, his blond hair covering his eyes. He was shirtless, and the dancing shadows of the bonfire animated his tattoos. "Total ankle snappers today, brah," he said to Stanton.

"I know. I was just gonna sit out there awhile."

"Forget that. There's some serious Barbies out here. You should hit up the party at Vanessa's house."

"I might stop by. I'm just gonna chill for a bit."

"All right, brother. See you there."

As Ted ran off, Stanton felt embarrassed for using the word *chill*. At thirty-four, he was hanging out with twenty-five-year-olds, trying to use their language. But that wasn't what bothered him the most. He tried his best not to adapt to their speech, not to use their cadences or expressions, but he'd found he couldn't do it. His mind melded to whatever group he was in, whether or not he wanted it to.

He ran into the water, the sprint exhilarating him and making his blood flow. When he was far enough out, he dove into the ocean and paddled. After about five minutes, he stopped paddling and looked back to shore, where the fires flickered in the darkness. What little light had remained of twilight disappeared, and night was fully descended. The moon lit the ocean a faint white, and he sat up on his board. He'd purposely forgone a wetsuit; he preferred the feel of the water directly against his skin. Even when he started shivering, there was something cathartic about it, as if he were shaking away the stresses he'd accumulated during the day.

Something rubbed his leg. His heart jumped into his throat, and he pulled his legs out of the water. Two shark attacks, one of them fatal, had occurred in this section of beach the year before. He'd never been concerned with sharks until he had witnessed an attack off the coast of Florida.

Stanton paddled back toward the bonfires on shore. There were no waves. He would come back early in the morning and hope to catch some then.

When he reached the shore, he looked down the beach and saw the lights on at Vanessa's house, where a party was just gearing up. He turned the other way, back to his apartment.

After showering, he sat on the balcony with his phone and dialed Melissa's number.

She answered on the second ring. "Hey."

"Hey. I missed your call yesterday. Sorry about that."

"It's okay. I saw the news. Are you all right?"

"As good as can be."

"He deserved it, Jon. If anybody did, he did."

"He was evil, but I'm having my doubts that we were up there for the right reasons."

"Why?"

"Honestly, I don't even know. Just a gut hunch, I guess."

"Your gut hunches are never just gut hunches. I would go with it."

He smiled. That was all he needed to hear. The loss of focus, the confusion, and the constant nausea he'd felt in his gut all went away with a few words from his ex-wife. There had been few moments after the divorce when he'd missed being married as much as he did right now.

"How are the boys?" was all he managed to say.

"They're good. They're at a sleepover right now."

"What? How could you—"

"Relax. I know your policy on sleepovers. But it's a sleepover with my parents."

"Oh, sorry. It's, um—"

"You don't need to explain. I know why. I would be a wreck seeing the things you see." There was a pause in the conversation, then she added, "That came out wrong."

"It's okay. I know what you meant." He took a deep breath, letting it out slowly before speaking again. "I miss you."

"I miss you, too."

"Then why can't we be together? I just don't get it, Mel. I know you love me."

"Of course I love you. That's not it. It's the not knowing. I send you off every day for fifteen hours, and I have no idea whether you're going to come back to me or whether someone's showing up at my door with an apology and a medal. And you're gone, and I'm supposed to be the strong wife with the two kids just getting by. Well, I'm not that, Jon. I can't be that."

"This is the only thing I'm good at. I do so much good here, Mel. More than any politician or doctor or lawyer, I do good."

"I know you do. But that's not you talking. That's Michael Harlow. You're a good father, a good husband, and a good professor. You still have your counseling license, and you've never even tried that. I bet you would be a great counselor, too. Let somebody else do *good* for a while."

"What do you want me to do? Just quit and dump my cases on someone else?"

"That's exactly what I want you to do. Right now. Take your badge and throw it out the window right now, Jon. Then pack your things and come home to your family. We can figure out everything else as we go."

He looked back at his badge on the coffee table. "I..."

"I know, Jon. I know." She sighed. "Call me tomorrow, okay?"

She hung up, and he put down the phone, not taking his eyes off his badge. He picked it up, running his fingers across the lettering. He went out to the balcony and held it over the edge. He looked down at the pavement below then back at the badge. The two bonfires on the beach had turned to four, and Vanessa's party was now packed with guests, whose cars lined the road around the house.

Stanton went back inside and tossed his badge on the couch. Then he shut his balcony door and went to bed.

10

Despite the early hour, the precinct was already noisy when Stanton walked in. A drunk in cuffs by the entrance was yelling about police brutality. Behind him, an old man had wet himself, and the urine was still running down his leg.

At the front desk, Vickie was starting her shift with coffee mixed with a shot of whiskey from a small flask hidden in a pocket of her handbag. He'd caught her filling it once and had never said anything to anyone, and she had liked him ever since.

"Who's the old man over there?" he asked.

"One of Childs's cases. He walked into a church and went to the pulpit and started masturbating."

"He doesn't look like he knows what's going on. Have you checked with Missing Persons?"

"For what?"

Stanton glanced down into her coffee cup and noticed it was nearly empty. "Never mind." He walked over to the old man and knelt to eye level since he was seated. "Hello."

"Hi," the old man said.

"Do you know where you are?"

"I'm... I'm visiting my nephew. I'm visiting my nephew in Fort Lauderdale, and he told me to come here and pick up his sister. That's why I need to get my keys." He looked around the precinct. "I don't see him here, but the man took my keys. The big black man took my keys."

"Do you know your name?"

He thought for a moment, then a smile parted his lips. "Lawrence, um, Lawrence... It's Lawrence."

"Okay, Lawrence, you stay right here for a minute." Stanton went back to his office. He sat at his desk and tried Childs's phone, but no one answered. His next call was to a female detective in Missing Persons named Georgia.

"Got a guy here, looks to be in his seventies, maybe even eighties. Says his name's Lawrence. I don't know if that's a first or last name, but someone would have reported him missing in the last twenty-four hours."

"Hang on... okay, we got a Thomas Welch Lawrence, reported missing this morning from La Jolla."

"What's his date of birth?"

"Um, July 2, 1932. That's gotta be him."

"Call back whoever reported it and tell them he's over here."

"You got it."

Stanton waited a few beats before he turned and pulled out the three files again and placed them on his desk, just as Childs walked in.

"What the hell you doin' here so early?"

"Cleaning up your baggage. Old man out there is Tom Lawrence. Someone's coming to pick him up."

"Thanks."

"Don't mention it."

"You doin' okay?"

"Yeah. Why?"

"You look tense, man. All stressed out'n shit, tied up in knots."

"You wanna give me a massage?"

"Ha, you couldn't handle this sweet chocolate, brother." Childs looked down at the files, but said nothing. "Come out with me today."

"Where?"

"Drug buy. Our hero's got a warrant out for rape and forcible sodomy, and I set up a buy for some weed. Gonna pop him on his porch in front of his buddies. Come with."

"I don't think so, Danny. I got a lot of work to catch up on."

"Pssh, bullshit. You can catch up on it later. Come with. It'll be fun. When's the last time you went out on a real bust?"

"If you insist, I'll come. But I'm not going to be very helpful."

"Just stand there and look pretty then." He turned to leave. "Going ASAP. Grab your vest."

The van was hot, and the air conditioner only cooled the two people seated up front. Stanton sat in the back with Childs and six members of SWAT, who were dressed in heavy black gear with thick helmets. Stanton and Childs wore simple Kevlar vests with their shields dangling on chains around their necks.

"SWAT's goin' in hot," Childs said. "As soon as the fucker answers the door, they're goin' in. Another unit's covering the back, so you just gotta cover the side door on the east side of the house."

"How many inside?"

"Just him and two friends. One of them's an informant, and the other's too stoned to do much, so I'm not expecting anything. Just cover the door, and we'll go get drunk afterward. Well, I'll get drunk, and you'll sit there and judge me."

"Sergeant Childs," the driver bellowed, "target acquired. Surveillance team saw him park and go in the residence."

"Anyone with him?"

"Negative, sir."

"All right. Let's do it."

The van came to a stop thirty feet from the house. They waited for the signal from surveillance, and the field commander gave both teams the green light. Stanton hopped out of the back of the van. Childs took point as the SWAT members silently climbed the porch steps and took positions on either side of the door. Stanton's heart was pounding so loud that he thought he could hear it in his chest. Many detectives were part of the gun culture, ex-military men who had come up through street patrol and SWAT or strike teams. He was an academic who didn't like guns. It was alien territory every time he went out, and this situation was no different.

Childs gave a signal indicating that SWAT should wait for his mark, and they lifted their rifles. Stanton went around the side of the old house across the lawn. A truck, its hood open, parts strewn around it, rested in the grass. He stationed himself behind it and pulled out his sidearm.

He kept his eyes on the door as he heard Childs knock.

From inside, someone yelled, "Who is it?"

Childs gave them the name he had been using. Stanton glanced away for a moment at an object that had caught his eye, something yellow and red with stripes. He did a double-take. It was a wagon—a child's wagon. There were kids inside the house.

"No," he shouted. "Danny, there's kids."

The door flew open, and Childs yelled at the top of his lungs. More yelling ensued, followed by the sound of boots on hardwood floors, then someone opened fire.

Stanton sprinted through the side door, breaking it open with his shoulder, into an empty kitchen. He heard more shots from the living room, then crying. He raced out of the kitchen and turned down a hallway.

Peeking out of a room was a young boy, tears streaming down his face. As if the scene were happening in slow motion, Stanton saw a SWAT officer turn the corner and raise his weapon. Stanton could see in his eyes that he didn't recognize that the boy was not a target. He was going to fire.

From the door next to the boy's, someone stuck out a gun and fired at the officer. The officer opened with his automatic rifle. Stanton leapt in the way, wrapping his arms around the boy, feeling the impact of hot slugs embed into his Kevlar as he hit the floor, covering the boy with his body.

The gun came out of the room again, and the officer fired, hitting the arm. A man fell into the hallway, and the SWAT officer shot him just behind the ear. Blood spattered over Stanton and the child.

"Hold your fire!" Childs was shouting. "Hold your fire!"

Stanton got to his knees and checked the child, who was pale and trembling. In shock. Childs turned the corner.

"What the fuck happened?"

Before he could think or answer, Stanton ran at the SWAT officer and tackled him around the waist. The officer brought up his rifle, and Stanton swung down with his elbow, catching the officer on the chin, in the exposed area underneath his helmet. The officer smashed the butt of his rifle into Stanton's jaw, knocking him onto his back. The officer jumped up and pointed his weapon at Stanton's face. Childs grabbed it and swung it away from him.

Stanton was about to rise when he noticed a sensation on his right side. He looked down to see blood pouring out between the straps of his vest.

11

Lexi Underwood stepped off the yellow bus near her friend Kalie's house and waved good-bye to the bus driver. Now that she was thirteen, she was allowed to ride the bus alone, something her mother hadn't allowed her to do last year. The other girls had teased her, and she'd never had the chance to sit next to Chad on the ride home. He was tall and cute and played baseball, and he'd once let her borrow his pencil in class.

Kalie ran out of her house, and her mother shouted for her to be back in an hour.

"Why weren't you at school?" Lexi asked.

"I was sick. But it's not bad. Just a sore throat." She looked down the street as the bus turned a corner and disappeared. "They're having baseball practice at Silver Ridge Park. You wanna go watch?"

"Who's gonna be there?"

"You mean is Chad gonna be there?" she said, grinning.

"Well is he?"

"I dunno. Let's go see."

They strolled down the sidewalk, and Lexi noticed that her friend was nearly skipping. She had seen Kalie sick before and guessed this wasn't one of those times.

"Hey, guess what?" Kalie said. "My parents are taking me to Hawaii this summer."

"No way."

"Yeah. We're staying with my older sister 'cause she lives there with her boyfriend. She said she was gonna teach me how to surf, and that there's sharks you can see even from the beach 'cause they're so big."

"Whoa. I wish I could go to Hawaii."

"Why don't you come?"

"Would your mom let me?"

"I'll ask her. But I heard her talking to my sister, and they said they need something to keep me busy so I don't get into trouble, so I'll tell them I won't get into trouble if you're there."

Lexi felt excited until she realized there was no way she would be going. Her father had lost his job recently, and money was tight. She couldn't afford new clothes for school this year, even though she had grown out of her old clothes. Her mother had taken her to a secondhand store and bought one pair of pants and a couple of shirts for just a few dollars.

She often heard her mom crying at night, and her dad would tell her that everything was okay and they would land on their feet. Lexi had started saving any money she could find. She'd even sold her CDs and her iPod, and she had over a hundred dollars under her mattress. She was going to surprise her mom with it one day when she was crying again.

"I don't think I can go."

"Why not?"

"Um, I don't know. I don't think my parents will let me."

Kalie was looking out at the street. "Who's that?"

Lexie saw a light-blue Volkswagen Beetle following them slowly. The windows were too dark to see inside, but it was keeping pace with them. She stared at it a long while, and its engine revved before it sped away down the street. It turned right at a stop sign and was gone.

"Weirdo," Kalie said. "My mom says a bunch of weirdoes live in the neighborhood. Like drug addicts and stuff."

"Where?"

Tires screeched on the road behind them, and the Beetle crept slowly toward them again. There was no one else on the street and no cars on the road. The Beetle took up the middle of the road, following just a little behind the girls. Then it peeled out and shot down the street.

"Leave us alone, asshole, or I'm calling my daddy to kick your ass," Kalie shouted.

The driver slammed on the brakes. Lexi inadvertently gasped and stopped walking. The two girls stood there, staring at the car.

"If it backs up," Lexi said, "we need to run."

They waited a few more moments, then the brake lights turned off, and the car made another right-hand turn at the stop sign.

The girls looked behind them to see if it would come back. They waited a long time, and when it didn't return, they resumed their walk toward the park.

12

Stanton woke up in the ambulance. He was calm and knew where he was. Speaking softly, the paramedic explained what had happened. Stanton could see red and blue lights flashing outside and knew that Childs was following them.

The ER at Scripps was well lit and clean, and a trauma nurse came in and spoke to the paramedics for a while. A man he guessed was a doctor came in and examined him for about five minutes. The nurse told him that Stanton was a police officer who'd been shot while on duty, and the doctor told her to cover his other patients while he spent more time with Stanton.

"Dangerous line of work." The doctor leaned over Stanton as he examined the wound on his side.

"Someone has to do it."

The doctor stood up straight, keeping one hand on Stanton's forearm. He was always amazed how light a doctor's touch could be.

"Well, I'm not seeing any hemorrhaging. I think someone's looking out for you. I'm going to need an X-ray just to be sure."

Another tech came in twenty minutes later, after the nurse had given him pain medication. Stanton was loopy but understood he was being carted away for X-rays. They placed him in a cramped room then turned and twisted him, making him hold a lead shield in front of his genitals to minimize their radiation exposure.

After the X-rays, he was taken back to the quiet of his room. He lay staring at the ceiling. The pain meds made him feel light and ethereal.

He thought of his grandfather. His father's father had been an abusive alcoholic, but his mother's father was a kind and gentle soul. His mother always told him they never had any money when she was growing up because her father, who owned his own business, often felt bad for the poor who came to him with their hats in hand, and he had given them whatever he could.

Childs walked in. He sat down on the stool and stared at Stanton as if he were a ghost.

"I don't know what to say."

"It wasn't your fault, Danny."

"I should'a cleared that house. I shouldn't've went in guns blazing like some damn Western." He exhaled loudly. "At least the doctor says you're good. The shot lodged between the Kevlar and your skin. Tore up the skin pretty good, but nothing serious. Didn't penetrate more than a quarter inch. Probably hurt like a sonofabitch, though, huh?"

"Detective Stanton?" A young man in a button-down shirt and a cap walked in, documents in his hand.

"Yes?"

"These are for you." He handed Stanton a few documents then turned to leave. "Consider yourself served."

Childs looked at the man then the documents. Before Stanton could say anything, Childs was on his feet and had the man by the collar. He slammed him up against the wall. "Here? You gonna serve him here!"

"This is where they told me he'd be," the man said, his voice trembling.

"Who? Who told you?"

"The receptionist at the police station."

Childs shoved him into the wall one more time then let him go. He ran out of the room and nearly knocked over the IV stand next to the bed.

Childs looked at Stanton. "What's the docs?"

Stanton folded the documents and placed them on the table next to the bed. "They're a summons and complaint. The police force, the city, the county and me are being sued for the death of

Darrell Putnam."

13

When Stanton stepped out of his hospital room, Sandra was waiting for him in the corridor.

She was wearing a black long-sleeved shirt and camo pants, her long blond hair clipped in the back. She wasn't wearing any makeup, but she looked just as beautiful as she always did.

"You have a nasty habit of standing in the way of bullets."

"It's my magnetic personality."

She grimaced. "Oh, that's terrible. You are just not funny."

"I'm hilarious. The world just isn't ready for my humor."

They went to the reception desk and checked out. He filled his prescriptions at the pharmacy on the main floor, and as they waited, she held his hand. When they got out to the car, she helped him in then hopped into the driver's seat.

The car backed up, and she peeled out of the hospital parking lot and onto 5th Avenue before turning onto Washington Street. The traffic was heavy, and she weaved between cars. At one point, she turned on her red and blues and sped along the shoulder.

Stanton watched the city pass by. His city. He tried so hard to keep it at arm's length, but that never worked. San Diego was in his blood. It was filled with equal parts madness and compassion, humanity and evil. Its heroes worked tirelessly for little or no pay and no recognition. In fact, they were usually despised by the very people they were attempting to help. Its villains, who were often considered paragons of the city, got plenty of admiration. Most people still knew the difference, but something was changing. People were growing either more foolish or blind to what was happening: the evil were becoming the good, and no one seemed to notice.

"I was going to take you skydiving next week," she said.

"Movies at my apartment will have to suffice."

"Oh, I don't think we'll have time for movies," she said, placing her hand on his thigh. "Something about a wounded man is a turn on."

He smiled. "You really are crazy."

Sandra turned and took a street through unfamiliar neighborhoods with cheap strip malls before reaching her house in Mission Hills. The new house had an interesting design of cubes and rectangles, and most of the walls were made of glass. Sitting at the top of a small hill, the structure overlooked the neighborhood.

"I love the house," Stanton said.

"You've never been here?"

"No."

"I could'a swore I brought you here one night."

"I don't think so. You dating another sex crimes detective?"

"No, I prefer my men religious and suicidal."

She unlocked the door and turned off the alarm before leading him into the living room. The house, decorated in silvers and blues with black carpet, reminded him of something a stylish vampire might pick out. A single teddy bear rested on the leather couch. Before even setting down her keys, she picked it up and placed it in a wicker basket in the dining room.

Stanton sat on the couch and looked out the large bay windows. In the valley below, many of the homes had Spanish tile roofs. The lawns were perfectly manicured; gleaming luxury cars, Hummers, and Range Rovers sat in the driveways, where the owners could show them off to the neighborhood rather than lock them in their garages.

"This house seems pricey," he said.

"It was my father's. He was a pretty famous criminal defense lawyer."

"What's he think about you becoming a cop?"

"He's okay with it, I guess. Says it's dangerous and people get burnt-out too soon."

"That's about what my dad said."

"Your dad was a psychiatrist, right?" She sat next to him, handing him a bottle of water to take his pain meds.

"Yeah. He told me that power corrupts, no matter how nobly it's applied."

"He thought being a cop would corrupt you?"

"I think he was saying if you're not careful, power can corrupt anybody."

She ran her fingers through his hair and down his neck, giving him goose bumps. "What's this lawsuit about?"

"How'd you know about it?"

"I got a call from the precinct, asking where you were because a process server was looking for you."

"Didn't they know they can accept for me?"

"Some new girl, I think. I told her where we were before thinking about it."

"It's Putnam's mother. She's brought a wrongful death claim against the county, me, and the force."

"Who's the lawyer?"

"Gary Coop."

"I know Coop. He was friends with my father. They played golf together. He's a snake. My father liked him but never trusted him. You need to be careful, Jon."

"It's just a civil suit."

"You don't sound worried enough about it."

"I have no control over whether she sues me or not, so there's no use worrying about it. I'll worry about the stuff I do have control over. Like making a sandwich. I'm starving."

She smiled and kissed him softly. "Your wish is my command." She went to the kitchen.

He followed her with his eyes then went to the dining room table and sat down. He watched her the entire time she was in the kitchen, and when she came over to him with his food, he pulled her onto his lap and kissed her from her neck all the way up to her ear. She giggled then pressed her lips to his.

14

Ransom Corvan Talano sat across from the weeping police officer in the small gray room. It was an interrogation room but wasn't designated as such. The blank walls held no decorations, and the linoleum floor and gray ceiling were simple. The door was thick gray steel, and the table and chairs matched it.

He slid the officer a box of tissues. He had not seen a grown man cry in a long time, and it fascinated him. He watched for as long as the officer allowed. After a few minutes, the officer looked up and wiped his tears before sitting up straight and taking a deep breath.

You're trying to recover some of your dignity, Ransom thought. *It's too late, my friend.*

"Lieutenant," the officer said, "I was just doing what I thought was right. I never intended for any of this to happen or to be a black mark on the uniform."

"Tell me your side of the story, Officer Hunt. I want to know it. I'm on your side, but you gotta give me something to take to them."

"It was just a normal bust. Some piece'a shit wetback—" Hunt looked at him. "You're not Mexican, are you?"

"No."

"It was just some wetback cocksucker. Estefan somethin'. We busted him for a DUI, and he said he had ten grand in cash in his trunk. If we took it and let him go on the DUI, he wouldn't say nothin'."

"So what'd you do?"

The officer looked away, and Ransom leaned forward and

took his hand.

"What'd you do?" Ransom asked softly.

"We took it. We split it. My wife needed a new car. We only got one car, and I can't afford another one. I got a kid that's starting college soon, and medical bills are piling up. The county keeps cutting our benefits and we're havin' to pay more ourselves. I thought, 'Who would miss it?' I wasn't thinking." He leaned forward. "This job is all I got, Lieutenant. Please, help me keep it."

Ransom smiled and stood up. He came around the table and patted his shoulder before leaning down and whispering in his ear, "My mother was Mexican, you piece of shit. And you're going to jail."

Ransom kissed the man on the head gently, like a priest absolving him of his sins, then left the room. He could hear the officer start crying again.

Another Internal Affairs investigator, Rodney Kloves, ran up to him with a file in his hand. He was sweating, his suit disheveled, his tie stained from whatever he had eaten that morning.

"New case. I think you need to see it," he said.

Ransom flipped open the file. A picture of Jonathan Stanton was pasted on the front inside cover. He looked up, a grin on his face. "Jon Stanton, the last man standing."

Kloves nodded. "He's being sued for wrongful death for that pedophile who jumped off the roof."

"That was two weeks ago. Why haven't I been called in before?"

"He was cleared, sir."

"What do you mean 'cleared'? I'm the one who tells him when he's cleared."

"It was an order from Assistant Chief Ho himself, sir."

"Order to who?"

"I don't know."

He slammed the file shut. "They wanna let him slide, and now they're sending it to me to cover their asses. Get Ho on the line in my office."

"Yes, sir."

Ransom walked slowly down the hall, his thoughts swirling. After stopping to get a drink from the fountain next to the drunk tank, he took the stairs to his second-floor office. Photos of him in various locations decorated the room. He displayed no photos of his second wife or the two boys he'd had with her, but there were a few of his first wife, who had left their eldest boy in his care. He stared at her photo for a moment, then his phone buzzed.

"Lieutenant Talano," he said.

"Lieutenant, this is Chin Ho. What the hell's going on? I was in a meeting."

"I'm sorry, sir. I just got a file placed on my desk, and I needed to discuss it with you briefly."

"So discuss."

"It's Jon Stanton, sir."

"What about it?"

Ransom cleared his throat. "My understanding was he was cleared of any misconduct for this incident."

"He was, but that was before we had all the facts."

"And what facts would those be, sir?" The slight pause told him he had overplayed his hand. "No disrespect, sir. It's just an unusual case. It shouldn't have even been in Sex Crimes. Child Abuse handles all sex cases involving kids under fourteen, and Homicide had a legitimate claim to it as well."

"I know. There were some... extenuating circumstances. It's a mess. There's a pending lawsuit. Regardless, it's your mess to clean up now, Lieutenant. Now, if that's all, I have to get back with the chief."

"Of course, sir. Thank you for your time."

Ransom hung up and leaned back in his chair. *The lawsuit. That's what this is about.* The county and police force were covering their asses. They wanted Ransom to find misconduct and hang Stanton out to dry. If they discovered that he wasn't acting within the scope of his employment, which was up to IAD to determine, they wouldn't have to pick up the tab for the

lawsuit. Stanton would be a hundred-percent liable.
Ransom smiled to himself as he opened the file.

15

Stanton woke in the middle of the night, soaked in sweat, his heart pounding. He suddenly realized that he had been sleeping on his back, and the burning pain of the wound had shocked him wide awake. He looked at the clock: 12:21 a.m. He rose and found his clothes.

Moonlight drifted through the open window, along with the symphony of crickets in the yard. Sandra's perfect body, her skin a milky white glow, was next to him, her hair coming down over the pillow like gold-white waves. She was more beautiful than any woman he had ever been with. But when he was with her, all he thought of was his ex-wife, Melissa. Something about familiarity won out over beauty or charm.

Stanton went to the window. Sandra's neighborhood was quiet and calm, and he could scarcely hear anything other than crickets. Most affluent neighborhoods were quiet, and he wondered if it was because their residents had fewer worries and were more prone to go to sleep earlier and sleep more soundly. Despite popular culture's warnings, money did solve most problems.

"Come back to bed." Sandra's voice was silky in the night, and hearing it soothed him.

He turned to her and kissed her forehead, tasting the salt on her skin. "I'll call you tomorrow."

"I'll be busy tomorrow, and so will you. But we have right now."

"I need to go somewhere for a while. Maybe I'll come back in a few hours."

"And where, Detective Stanton, do you need to be that is more important than here?" She sat up in bed, revealing perfect breasts. The ends of her hair came down over them and danced on her nipples.

He kissed her one more time and left.

It was one thirty in the morning by the time Stanton had changed into a wetsuit and gotten into the warm Pacific. He paddled out much farther than he usually did at night then lay on his board, flat on his belly so as not to put pressure on his back. He checked the ankle strap that tethered him to the board, then he slid off and held his breath. Facedown in the ocean, he opened his eyes, feeling the sting of the salt. The moonlight illuminated the surface, but farther down, the water turned a deep blue then black, creating a bottomless pit of darkness where things from nightmares roamed, looking for prey. He flipped over onto his back and stared up at the stars. The waves were nonexistent, and the water was calm. He felt as if he could fall asleep. *I should try that sometime.* He knew he never would—hypothermia would kill him before he awoke.

The salt water had dribbled into his wetsuit and was soaking through the bandage, burning the wound. He felt it run across his back, down his legs, and up into his head. The pain melted with him, became one with him. He could control it, turn it off and on like an electric circuit.

He thought about Putnam and that last look he'd given him. *I didn't do it.*

In the recesses of his mind, Stanton knew it was true. Whoever killed those girls was still out there—still hunting. The next one chosen would be a blonde, athletic girl of ten to thirteen years old. Her parents, who would still be together, would be poor or middle class, not rich. She would be on her own a lot while both parents worked. She would be beautiful, naïve, trusting of others, and always willing to help. That would be what he exploited—her willingness to give directions, open a door, or help a total stranger move a box.

And if Stanton didn't find him first, she would die.

16

The next morning, Stanton got to the precinct around nine. A new officer, a woman, was manning the front desk. He stopped and looked around for the old receptionist but didn't see her. In his office, the three files he needed were already open. He booted up his computer and pulled up a document: a map of the three victims' homes with Putnam's mother's house right in the center. It was so easy. Stanton and Childs had simply run a search for registered sex offenders in the area and hit Putnam. Solutions to sex crimes were never that easy, and Stanton knew it—he'd always known it. But he wished, just this once, that it was.

He'd never dreamt he would find himself investigating sex crimes, especially sex crimes against children. He was a homicide detective who had always seen himself as a homicide detective. With sex crimes, the victims were still alive. The horrible interviews with broken and bleeding women haunted him in the quiet hours of night. Though he refused to admit it to himself, he was glad he wouldn't have those interviews with the three victims he had now.

Still, he didn't understand why these homicides were assigned to Sex Crimes, but he didn't care to ask. He wanted this case, had wanted it the moment he heard about it.

"What the hell are you doing back?" Childs said as he walked in.

"Have some things I need to finish up on."

"Are you shitting me? You were shot. Get the hell outta here. I ain't kiddin'. I'm not watching you bleed out all over your desk."

"I will. Just need a couple of hours."

He shook his head. "People think I'm the crazy one, but I think you've got some serious issues."

As Childs left, Stanton rose and shut his door before turning back to the files. He picked up Sarah Henroid's file and a disk dropped out. He gazed at the disc a moment then popped it into his computer. His media player opened to a shot of the interior of a house.

The person holding the camera was in the kitchen, and Stanton could hear laughter. The camera turned to the right and caught a glimpse of a woman in a striped shirt and jeans, setting a table. Balloons and ribbons were up around her. Behind her, a banner read *Happy Birthday, Sarah*. Stanton counted the candles on the cake: ten. A young girl came into view, and the family began to cheer. She waved to the camera as the voice behind it—Stanton knew it was her father's from the interviews he'd done with him—asked what she wanted for her birthday.

"A baby sister."

The father turned to the wife and said, "Maybe we should get working on that tonight, honey?"

"Jack!" she said, turning red.

He laughed, and she shook her head as she continued setting the table while several other children came in from the living room.

Stanton turned it off. He felt embarrassed for them, embarrassed that they had been forced to share such a tender moment with him, in this place, at this time. Stanton sat silently, staring at nothing in particular to clear his head. After a few minutes, he flipped it back on.

Sarah took her place in front of the cake, a wide grin over her face. Jack led them all from behind the camera in singing "Happy Birthday." Then she blew out the candles in one blow. The mother began cutting up the cake and asked for Jack's help. The video ended, turning to a blue screen with numbers on it. Stanton took out the disk and slipped it back into its jacket in

the file.
I'm so sorry.

Stanton spent the morning on the beach, lying around. He read a book on the psychopathology of sex abuse for a while, then ate tacos and drank a Diet Coke from a roach coach parked near the beach. His back ached and burned, and he went into the water to cool it off, but that didn't help. Finally, he went back to his apartment, took his pain meds, and fell asleep on the balcony.

He woke around two in the afternoon. He showered, dressed, and headed out the door to his car.

The Fillmore Elementary parking lot was full, so he came to a stop between two rows of cars. He sat quietly until someone came out of the school and freed up a parking spot.

It was a hot, bright day, and he put on his sunglasses as he got out of the car. The elementary school had already let out, but crowds of people were gathered on the soccer field. Two teams of young girls were battling it out on the field while the coaches on the sidelines shouted instructions.

The male coach wore the blue-and-gold colors of the home team. Stanton strolled over to him and stood quietly as the coach finished prepping the players waiting to go in.

He saw Stanton, and held his gaze.

"I'm sorry about popping in like this, Doug."

"I saw the news. You should've called me first. I don't think I should've heard it like that."

"I'm sorry. The past couple weeks have been a blur."

He said something to one of the girls and then turned back to Stanton. "I'm glad you got him and that he's gone. Truth be told, I wanted to be there when they convicted him. To look in his eyes and tell him I'll see him in hell and that we'd finish it there. But I'm glad it ended the way it did."

Stanton looked out over the field, watching the girls as they ran to one end of the field, where a player from the visiting team stole the ball and tripped another player. The girls argued, and the referee had to break it up.

"I need to be sure it was him, Doug," Stanton said. "The evidence pointing to him is circumstantial. I haven't closed the cases yet because I'm still looking into it."

"The news said his mother said he did it."

"His mother has dementia. I'm not sure she knew that we were talking about these recent cases. She could easily have thought we were talking about the cases he was already convicted for."

Doug Henroid took a deep breath, watching the action on the field. He withdrew two of his players and sent in replacements. "For the first time, I found some peace with this... at least as much as a father could. Why are you telling me this?"

"Because I need your help. There's three girls attributed to Putnam, and I think there's a connection there we're missing."

"I told you last time—Sarah didn't know those other two girls."

"Is there any chance she had a circle of friends you didn't know about? A group or club she belonged to and you didn't really check up on? Anything like that?"

"No."

"She got straight As in school. Did she belong to any study groups or anything?"

"Not that I can recall. I know she got tutoring in math, but that was always a tough subject for her."

Stanton scanned his memory of the case. Since his youth, he could recall, as clearly as video, things he'd seen. And he could rewind and replay it in his head, like a DVD. From what he remembered, no one had ever mentioned a tutor.

"What was this tutor's name?"

"Um, I don't know. You'll have to call my wife. She handled all that stuff."

Stanton gave him one of his cards, though he knew Doug had at least five or six at home. "If you think of anything else we haven't discussed, call me anytime, Doug."

"I will."

He turned to leave and was nearly hit by a soccer ball. One of the girls picked it up and whispered under her breath, "Watch where you're going."

He went back to the car and dialed the number for Sarah's mother.

"Hello?"

"Mrs. Henroid?"

"Yes."

"This is Detective Jon Stanton. How are you, Betty?"

There was a slight pause. "I'm fine."

"I just spoke to Doug. He told me that Sarah was taking tutoring lessons in math. I was wondering if I could get the name and number of that tutor."

"What for?"

"Just tying up some loose ends."

"Okay, well, hang on… okay, you ready?"

"Yeah."

"Her name's Tracey Adams. She lives in La Jolla. I just texted you the number. Do you have it?"

"Got it. Thanks."

She hung up without saying good-bye.

Stanton dialed the precinct and gave his call-in code. He asked dispatch to run a check on Tracey Adams in La Jolla. He pulled out and was heading back to his apartment when dispatch called with an address in La Jolla near the beach. It was fifteen minutes from his location.

He took the interstate, his windows down to let the wind run between his fingers, up his arm, and through his hair. The interstate was packed, though it wasn't rush hour. The city seemed to be getting more crowded.

Tracey Adams lived in an upscale neighborhood filled with mansions, where the occupants scarcely used the space they had. Their waste was a statement saying that they had so much money it was practically valueless to them. The ultra-wealthy usually showed disdain for money as a way to prove to others they had a lot of it.

At the address was a large, three-story white home with manicured lawn and hedges. Its driveway looped around a fountain and back out to the road. He came to a stop at the curb and got out.

The neighborhood was quiet, except for two children at the end of the block riding bicycles. The ocean was just far enough away to give the air a crisp, clean smell but not close enough to dampen it. He walked to the front door and knocked.

A woman with bleached blonde hair, wearing a tennis outfit, answered the door. "Yes?"

Stanton flashed the tin. "Jon Stanton. I'm with San Diego PD. Is Tracey Adams home?"

"What do you want with her?"

"I just need to ask her a few questions about one of the students she was tutoring."

Her initial surprise turned to anger. "It's about that little whore who went missing, isn't it? Well, you can't talk to Tracey. I'm her mother, and I'm not giving you permission to talk to her. You can just call our lawyer and talk to him."

She slammed the door in his face. Technically, she had the right to refuse. Interviewing any child under the age of fourteen required parental consent, and Tracey was thirteen years old. He went back to his car and asked dispatch for the nearest middle school. Then he cancelled that and asked them to find the nearest private school.

It was the Huntington Academy, eight miles north of La Jolla.

17

As Stanton drove back to the interstate, he thought about his last visit to Huntington Academy. He'd been working a homicide case, and he'd gone there to inform a twelve-year-old girl that her mother wasn't coming home.

The woman's ex-boyfriend's stalking had escalated to murder. Stalking cases, though they were treated initially as misdemeanors, were some of the most dangerous cases in the entire criminal justice system. The suspects were, as a rule, deeply disturbed and had violent fantasies without any correlation to reality. They were always the most indignant as well, unable to understand why they were being treated so badly when they had done nothing wrong. They were also the most likely to cross the line between fantasy and reality and harm the objects of their obsession.

The Huntington Academy was situated on two acres of lush property, an oasis in the middle of the steel and concrete city. It was old brick with stained-glass windows and massive wooden doors that had been intricately carved with scenes from the Bible. Originally founded as a monastery, the building had been converted to a Catholic school over seventy years ago.

Stanton went in. There was always something odd about being in a school later in the afternoon, when everyone had left. As a youth, he'd spent lots of late afternoons in school for detention. He wasn't poorly behaved, he simply didn't do anything; no assignments, no participation and no discussions. The teachers were unsure how to deal with him, and they assumed he was being intentionally disobedient. Looking back on it, he knew the cause of his behavior was a deep depression that had followed him through his life. It affected him so intensely that he lost track of where he was and what he was doing. His schoolteachers had never recognized it.

He poked his head into the administration office, where an older woman was filing documents. Framed photos of the school's headmasters were up on the walls, and a large painting of the Pope graced the other room off to the right.

"Hi," he said, pulling out his badge. "I need to see the school police officer."

"He may have already gone home. Let me check." She pressed the button on a phone at the counter, and after three rings, a gruff male voice answered.

"Yeah?"

"Steve, I have another police officer from the... ah—where are you from, Officer?"

"Sex Crimes Division of San Diego PD."

She paused. "Did you get that?"

"Yeah, be right down."

She hung up the phone, and Stanton could see she was struggling over whether it was appropriate to ask for details.

"It's just something routine," Stanton said. "Tying up some loose ends. Nothing to worry about."

"Oh, I was wondering." She sounded relieved. "Officer Gage should be down in just a few minutes."

"Thanks."

Stanton waited out in the hallway. He perused the photos in the trophy case outside the administration office. They showed kids from first grade through twelfth grade, wearing uniforms, many for non-traditional sports like water polo and cricket.

"What can I help you with, Officer?"

Stanton turned to see a giant with a gray handlebar mustache. He was easily close to seven feet tall and carried a massive belly that hung over his belt. The tips of tattoos poked down past the man's sleeves. He stood close to him, and Stanton knew instantly that the officer was attempting to establish dominance. *He's hiding something.*

"Detective," Stanton corrected.

The officer folded his arms. "What is it I can do for you?"

Stanton saw the office secretary staring at them, attempting to listen in. "Can we talk somewhere private?"

"I guess. Come back to my office."

He followed the officer down the hall and up a flight of stairs. The hallways on the second floor were filled with lockers and posters announcing dances or fundraisers. A couple of election signs for student body president and vice president candidates hung among the other posters.

"I'm Jon, by the way."

"Henry."

He stopped at a cramped room squeezed between a classroom and a drinking fountain. The desk and chairs barely fit into the space. A photo of a SWAT team was up on the wall, the signatures of all the members along the bottom. A certificate of excellence from the California Board of Education was posted behind the desk.

Stanton shut the door though Henry hadn't asked him to.

"So what brings you here, Detective?"

"I need to speak to you about one of the students here. Tracey Adams."

"What about her?"

"You know her?"

"There's only three hundred kids here. I know everyone."

Stanton nodded and glanced up to the SWAT poster again, noticing that Henry was the one second from the left. "She was a tutor for a young girl who went missing three months back. Sarah Henroid. Sarah didn't go to this school."

"Yeah, I remember. There was a staff meeting about it."

"Really? Why?"

"Just to talk about it. Tracey told a bunch'a the kids, and they was thinking to hold some discussions in the classrooms. Help the kids understand it a little better."

"Did they?"

"I don't know. We never had the discussions. None'a the kids seemed to care too much. People go missing all the time, I guess."

"Did Tracey ever say anything about Sarah to you directly?"

"Say anything like what?"

"Anything at all. This is the first I've learned about Sarah having a tutor, and I'm just trying to get a handle on their relationship."

Nodding, Henry sucked in air through his teeth. "I get what this is. You think maybe Tracey knows somethin' about Sarah disappearing. Well, Detective, anything the students tell me is confidential. I can't tell you about the conversations we've had."

He's been here too long, Stanton thought. *He's forgotten that he's a police officer and thinks he's the school security guard now.*

Stanton had seen numerous school officers find comfort in the predictability of their positions and request to stay. There was no such confidentiality between officer and student, but the conviction with which Henry said it made Stanton think the man actually believed it.

A NASCAR cup with coffee stains around the lip sat on his desk, with a calendar up on the wall behind it. Four nights this week were circled. Stanton thought that he was probably moonlighting as a security guard or bouncer.

"Henry, I went to Tracey's mother, and she slammed the door in my face and told me to talk to her lawyer. That lawyer probably makes more in a month than I do all year. I'm just a worker bee, trying to close out this case so I can tell the parents I did everything I could. I understand you got a good setup here and you don't want to piss anybody off. But if you can give me anything, I would certainly appreciate it."

The expression on Henry Gage's face told Stanton he was debating something. When Henry's face softened, Stanton knew he had reached a decision.

"Her mom's a real bitch. I busted Tracey for truancy once, and her mom went to the headmaster and tried to get me fired." He exhaled loudly and leaned back in his seat. "Tracey's a fucked-up girl. I caught her a few months back sellin' dope to the younger kids behind the school."

"Did you file a report?"

"Hell, yes, I filed a report. Her big-time lawyer got the charges dropped to an infraction with a fine. She was suspended for a week, and that was it."

"By the time they're selling, kids are usually heavy drug users."

"Ain't no different with her. Used to be just pot, I think, but she's moved on into the heavier stuff. She talks sometimes and doesn't make sense. I heard from some other people she buys her dope from some *chivato* on Lincoln Street uptown."

"Did she get Sarah involved in it?"

He bit his upper lip. "What I'm gonna tell ya, you didn't hear from me."

"Of course."

"They got parties, these kids. And they ain't like the parties you and me had growin' up. They got these sex parties. All the kids go and get drunk and get high and fuck around. One kid I know here that opens up to me says a guy might have sex with four or five different girls in one party."

"What's that got to do with Sarah?"

"She was at them parties with Tracey."

"She was ten."

"I know."

"Are you telling me ten-year-olds are having sex parties?"

"I don't know about havin' 'em, but they definitely goin' to 'em."

Stanton looked down at his shoes, remembering himself at ten. "When I was that age, I used to play baseball until nine every night, and my parents wanted me home at eight. That was about the most trouble I got into."

"I used to steal my older brother's porno mags. But it's a different world now, Detective. Kids ain't kids no more."

"No, I guess not." He looked at the American flag about the

size of a dinner plate hanging behind the desk. "Is there anything else you can tell me, Henry? Anything that might help me find out if Sarah got involved in some things that were over her head?"

"Tracey's your best bet. You might be able to convince her mom to let you talk to her."

"How?"

"She was the one allowing the kids to have them parties at her house."

Stanton took out his notepad and made a few notes before standing to leave. "We never spoke as far as I'm concerned."

"Appreciate it."

Stanton walked to the door and turned before leaving. "Out of curiosity, who was Tracey's lawyer?"

"Gary Coop."

18

Calvin Riley parked his Volkswagen Beetle in front of the United Studios of Modern Mixed Martial Arts on Sports Arena Boulevard. He finished his energy drink and then grabbed his gym bag and went inside.

He sauntered past the cage and the weight-room and put his things in his locker. He stopped at the full-length mirror in the locker room and hit a few bodybuilding poses before heading out to the bag area. His pectoral muscles bulged underneath his tight shirt.

Several heavy bags and speed bags were set up around the space above blue mats on the floor. He wrapped his hands tightly then slipped on bag gloves before stretching and warming up with a little shadowboxing. Then he went to work.

The bag responded to his blows lightly at first as he just tapped it. He worked his simpler combos. *Jab, left hook. Left hook, right hook. Left hook, left uppercut.* He felt his muscles warming as sweat formed on his forehead. When he was ready, he increased his speed, and the combos became more complex. The bag started to move and, soon, bend to his blows.

He rained down combos one after another, then worked in kicks and knees. Calvin moved seamlessly from one motion to the next and from one stance to the next. Being ambidextrous, he was as comfortable in orthodox as southpaw stance. His breathing was slow and purposeful—in through his nose in long breaths, and out his mouth in quick, short ones. He flexed his abdomen, training himself to accept body blows when striking.

The minutes turned to two hours, and his hands ached. The

skin on his knees had been scraped raw, and blood trickled down his legs. He stopped to check the clock. He still had energy, and he had to get all of it out if he wanted to sleep. He unwrapped his hands and went to the cardio room where he hopped on a treadmill. He took it slow at first, until his leg muscles adapted, then he pushed it up to ten miles per hour. His eyes forward, he felt the sweat pouring out of him, soaking his shirt and shorts.

After another hour of running, he was finally exhausted. He fought back the vomit in his throat as he stepped off the treadmill. He went to his gym bag and got out his sports drink and a protein bar. Then he took a seat next to the cage, where a jujitsu class was practicing lion-killer chokes from the back mount.

A large man in a tank top stepped up to him. "You hoppin' in, Riley?"

"Just watching today."

"Well, you let me know if you wanna hop up there and crack some skulls. We got a tournament coming up, and my boys need some practice."

"Williams is gonna win, but Larson's weak on the ground."

He nodded. "Don't suppose it would do any good to ask you to fight for us?"

"I'm not interested in attention."

"Hell, fight under a different name. Call yourself the Wrecker or Fist of Fury or some shit."

"Maybe later. But I'll sit this one out for now."

The coach sat next to him. "What's goin' on, Riley? You one tough motherfucker, and you don't do nothin' with it. You in here every night, and I ain't never seen you hang out with any'a the boys. Did you go out to the clubs with Lonnie and them this weekend?"

"No."

"We're a team up in here, Riley. I know we got weekend warriors that come in and train for a few months and take off, but you been with me damn near four years. How old are you now?"

"Twenty-three."

"Ain't right for someone your age not to be goin' and gettin' some pussy with the boys. You gonna grow up like me and get a wife and settle down one day, and you gonna miss these times, man. I'm tellin' ya."

"I know. I know it's a team here, and I want to take part in it. I'll make more of an effort."

He slapped Calvin's arm. "All right, then."

After the coach left, Calvin rose and finished the rest of his drink in a few gulps. He threw the protein bar in the trash, grabbed his gym bag, and left.

It was dark and the moon was out, a bright glowing orb in a black sky. He took Loma Boulevard down to Ocean Beach Park and found a relatively secluded area. He parked and took off his shoes. The sand was still warm from the sun, and he stood still a long time, his toes buried in the sand. Then he walked over to the edge of the water and sat down, just far enough away that the crackling waves broke in front of him, tickling the tips of his toes before sliding back to the sea.

He loved the ocean at night, the way the moon lit up the surface. He often went surfing late, at two or three in the morning when everyone else had gone home. He would wade into the white surface, lie flat on his back, and stare at the moon.

An odd sense of nostalgia coursed through him; the moon had been full the night he killed his grandparents. He wondered if the moon had anything to do with that. He was only eleven when he'd shot them both in the head while they were sleeping. Afterward, he'd gone and sat on the porch, where he waited for his mother to get home. He remembered the sense of calm clearly. The porch had been cold—they were living in Minnesota at the time—but he didn't wear a coat, and he'd regretted it. His mother spent thousands of dollars and took nearly three years to seal his juvenile record. She was always fighting for him to have a normal life. They had moved to California for a fresh start.

Mother.

He checked his watch. It was 11:00 p.m. Calvin jumped to his feet and ran back to his car. He started the engine before he even had his seatbelt on. He peeled out in reverse then shot forward, toward the San Diego Freeway. The streets were clear, except for the occasional drunk weaving in and out of the lanes in front of him. He shot past them then cut them off, seeing if they were drunk enough to crash. None of them were.

He got off the freeway at Laredo Drive, and the trip home took only another ten minutes. His house was large, far larger than his parents' income should have afforded. But his grandfather had inherited it and passed it on to Calvin's mother in his will.

Calvin parked and sat in the car, the night quiet around him. His mother peeked through the curtains, and he saw his two little brothers sitting at the dining room table. She often kept the whole family up when Calvin stayed out too late. His father was the only one who wouldn't stay up. Calvin took a deep breath and opened the door.

The night was cool, and the freeway and main road were far enough away that he couldn't hear the traffic. All he could hear was the buzz of an airplane flying overhead. His heart beat fast and he wanted to stall, but this was something that grew worse the more he put it off.

He went inside. The kitchen light was on, and he stood just outside the linoleum. His mother was standing over the stove, cooking soup.

"Where were you so late?" she said, not looking up from her pot.

"At the gym."

"That gym closes at ten."

"I went to the beach and lost track of time. I'm sorry, Mama."

"You're sorry?" she said, her voice rising in pitch. "You're sorry? Your poor brothers have been here without food for hours, and you're sorry?"

"I never said not to eat when I wasn't here, Mama."

She stood silently a moment before turning back to her pot.

Calvin relaxed, thinking it was over. He turned to leave then felt the scalding soup over his head. It burned his eyes and the soft skin on his neck, and he screamed and fell to the floor. His mother lifted the pot and slammed it down over his head, shouting to his brothers not to turn away from it. One blow caught him in the back of the head, and he saw flashes of light.

"No, Mama," he said, crying. "Mama, stop. Please, Mama, stop."

Calvin heard the kitchen table being pushed across the bare linoleum then the latch on the door leading to the cellar.

"Get your ass in there, boy."

He got to his knees, wiping at the hot liquid drizzling down his face. The three-by-three-foot opening in the floor had wooden stairs that descended almost a dozen feet. He had spent most of his childhood there, or in places like it. He had once feared the dark and quiet, but not anymore, not since he was ten years old.

He crawled down the stairs, and his mother kicked his feet in, causing him to slide down a few steps. He looked up at her, feeling his face swelling, and she slammed the door. He heard the table pushed back over the latch, then the house went quiet.

Calvin made his way down to the cement floor, which was cold but welcoming. He knew every crack, fracture, bump, and chip. He followed one crack to the right, which led to the wall, and curled up against it. He took off his shirt and pressed it to his face and neck, then wept quietly in the dark.

19

The residents of Ocean Beach Park were fiercely protective of their local businesses, parks, playgrounds, and even the surfers. Outsiders were regarded with a suspicious eye the moment they stepped on the sand, and Stanton had been no different. Things had even come to blows one night when one of the local surfers had slid across the bottom of Stanton's wave, knocking him off his board. Stanton was willing to forget it, but he knew that if he did, he could never surf this beach again. The locals would have seen him as weak and never allowed him back.

The local man had been a thick Hawaiian named Kekoa. When Stanton came in to shore, he'd found him with a group of people near the cars. He walked by casually, as if he hadn't noticed him, and Kekoa had turned away just long enough for Stanton to rush him. He could still replay it in his mind as if he were watching a bout blow-by-blow as it happened: He threw his arms around Kekoa's waist and took him down. Kekoa wrapped his legs around Stanton, trying to squeeze out the last of his breath, but Stanton jammed his elbow into the man's throat and pushed down with his bodyweight. Kekoa spun Stanton's arm away and put his hands around Stanton's throat. Stanton twisted his neck to the side then bit down on the fleshy part of Kekoa's hand, hard enough to tear the flesh and draw blood. Kekoa had been distracted enough that Stanton landed a couple of elbows into his nose.

They'd been pulled apart seconds afterward, but it was enough. Stanton had shown that even though Kekoa could clearly come out on top in a brawl, he was going to get hurt, maybe even hurt bad, in the process. Kekoa, and the other surfers, stayed away from Stanton after that.

Stanton felt the pressure shift in the water. The wave was only ten feet behind him now, and he began to paddle toward shore as the water lifted him higher. When he was nearly at the zenith of the wave, he jumped to his feet.

The wave pushed him toward shore with such speed that the wind howled in his ears. He pushed his board to the right, cutting across the wave and leaving a thin streak of white foam, then cut back in the other direction. He crouched low enough that his fingertips touched the surface of the wave, dipping into the sea as if they belonged there. He rode in with his fingers in the water.

The wave dissipated, and he jumped off the board into a few feet of water and carried it back to shore over his head. He stuck the board in the sand then collapsed next to it, looking up at the moon that radiated white light like a bulb dangling from the sky. The sound of tires screeching broke the peace of the moment. He saw a Volkswagen Beetle tearing out of the parking lot farther down the beach.

He turned back to the sea and watched the waves come. Twenty or so surfers were still out there, catching wave after wave, hoping each set would be the one they could go back to their parties and talk about, the one that flung them twenty feet or dragged them under and nearly drowned them.

After toweling off, he picked up his cell phone, which he'd stashed underneath his towel, and dialed Melissa's number. She answered quickly.

"I hear waves. You at the beach?"

"Yeah, I've really gotten into night surfing now. You and the boys should come out with me."

"You know I don't surf."

"I could teach you."

"Like how you taught me to drive a stick?"

"That crappy seven-hundred-dollar car was all I had, and

you nearly destroyed the transmission. We had to stop."

She laughed softly. "I'll never forget your face after the first few times we heard that awful grinding sound. You were sweet to let me keep trying as long as you did."

He looked up at the sky. "I wish you could see the moon the way I'm seeing it now. It's so clear, it feels like it's taking up the whole sky."

"I'm lying in bed. I can see it through the window. Is it true more crimes happen during full moons?"

"Yes."

"Why?"

"I don't know. The moon seems to have some sort of psychological effect on us, but science hasn't caught up to superstition yet."

The silence between them lasted a few seconds, then she sighed. "I miss you."

"I miss you, too."

"Are you coming to pick up the boys this weekend?"

"Yeah. I'd like for you to come with us. I thought maybe we'd hit the zoo."

"I can't. I have to work. One of the girls quit, and I was given all her properties. It's nice 'cause it's so much more money, but I don't like having to work on the weekends."

Stanton counted three waves as they sat quietly on the phone. But it wasn't an awkward silence, more like a silence bred from the comfort they felt with each other. "I better go. I just wanted to talk to you right now."

"Okay. Be careful, Jon."

After he hung up, he grabbed his board and headed back to his apartment. It was Friday night and there was a line of cars on the street, all headed to beach parties that had barely gotten underway. A car packed with girls hollered at him as he crossed the street, and he waved.

When he got back to his building, a man in a gray suit was sitting in one of the chairs in the lobby. The man, who looked familiar, rose as Stanton came in. He spit his gum into an ashtray before walking over.

"Detective Stanton," he said, holding out his hand, "Lieutenant Ransom Talano. Pleasure, Detective. I've heard a lot of good things."

Stanton shook his hand. "Have we met before?"

"No, not that I'm aware of. I'm just doing some follow-up on the Darrell Putnam case. I'm sure you know by now the family's filed a lawsuit, so I've just been assigned to make sure all the t's are crossed. You know how it is."

"I didn't know that's all IAD did—just cross t's."

Talano was silent a moment before saying, "Why would you think I'm with IAD?"

"Your firearm's on your left side, but you shook with your right and threw out your gum with your right. Most officers keep their firearm on the side of their dominant hand for a controlled draw. The only division I know that doesn't is IAD, because it's annoying to bump your firearm while filling out paperwork."

He smiled and pointed his index finger at Stanton. "You're good. I heard as much. 'One of the best on the force' is what everyone keeps telling me."

"Why are you here, Ransom? Is it to give me rope to hang myself? If it is, at least come upstairs so I can get a drink. I'm dying of thirst."

Stanton went to the elevators, and Ransom reluctantly followed. They were silent on the ride up, and when they got into his apartment, Stanton pulled a bottle of orange juice from the fridge and poured two glasses. He handed one to Ransom, then sat on the couch. The bay doors were open, letting in the salty ocean breeze. He could hear the teenagers honking, laughing, and shouting eleven floors below.

"I know what you want, Ransom." Stanton knew he probably preferred to be called "Lieutenant," but he continued to use Talano's first name, putting them on an even playing field. "But you're not going to find it. The incident was clean. There was probable cause and a warrant for his arrest. I was just trying to bring him in, and he chose to jump instead. The only way to challenge it is to challenge the warrant, and that's gonna piss off Judge Gilligan. He's known as being temperamental and doesn't like when people second-guess him. Doesn't seem like the kind of guy I would want to piss off."

"You're Mormon, aren't you?"

Stanton sipped his orange juice. Ransom was good—he had immediately put Stanton back on the defensive—but Stanton didn't take the bait. He simply responded, "Yes."

"Now, I heard Mormons believe they're going to be gods one day, that you all are polytheists. A lot of people—not me, mind you, but a lot—would say that's not Christian. What do you say when people tell you that?"

"I don't say anything. Everyone's entitled to their opinions. Religion's just about comfort in death anyway. Everything else is just details."

"Details? *Details*. It's all in the details, Detective. Everything's important. Haven't you learned that yet?"

"No. I'm more of a big-picture guy."

Ransom took a sip of his juice and raised his eyebrows. "Good juice."

"I make it myself. It's orange and clementines."

He drank half the glass then placed it on a coaster on the coffee table. "I like your apartment. The view of the ocean alone is enough to make the rent worthwhile. How much do you pay here, if you don't mind me asking?"

"I do mind, actually."

Ransom smiled softly then finished the rest of his juice, not taking his eyes off Stanton. "Well, Detective, I can see that everything is probably in order, like you said. Seems I would be just spinning my wheels here."

He rose, and Stanton walked him to the door. He held it open as Ransom stepped out without a word.

As Stanton shut the door, he thought for the first time that he might want to call his union lawyer. Ransom was too good. Even the time and place he'd chosen for the initial meeting—

his apartment, late at night, after he was relaxed from surfing—showed that he was careful and had insight into people's weaknesses.

Internal Affairs detectives, the good ones anyway, were cut from the same cloth: obsessed with rooting out corruption. But occasionally, that obsession crossed the line into that gray area where some cops lost themselves. Stanton decided he would give his lawyer a call. Ransom Talano was dangerous.

The second Ransom heard Stanton's door shut behind him, he bit his hand so hard he broke the top layer of skin. Then he kicked the garbage can by the elevators, and when the elevator dinged and opened, an old lady with a little dog saw him and was startled. He smiled as widely as he could to cover up the anger pouring out of him, but she just looked down at the floor and stepped past him.

He rode the elevator, feeling foolish about letting his emotions get the better of him. At the same time, he felt a rush, and it put a smile on his face. Most officers, even seasoned homicide detectives, became stammering teenagers during an IAD investigation. They responded with pure emotion: either absolute anger or total despair. Many cried; some grew so enraged they would throw things or threaten his life. The reaction was always dramatic enough that, after the dust settled, Ransom had them where he wanted.

But Jon Stanton was different. He was calm and even, seemingly unafraid. Ransom even thought that Stanton might actually have believed he'd done nothing wrong. One thing was for certain, though: he wouldn't be giving IAD any help.

There has to be another way to get to him.

Ransom got outside, and a waft of ocean air hit his face, making him nauseated. He had never enjoyed the sea. Some of the other detectives in IAD went boating every other weekend, but he never joined them. It reminded him too much of bathing.

He noticed a nearby diner. It looked like a dive, and the surfboard up over the entrance had the words "Big Kahuna's" painted on it in bright red, lit up with Christmas lights. He went to his car, got Stanton's file, and headed to the diner.

The interior was in worse shape than the exterior, and the place was filled with the smell of roasting pork, burnt onions, and peppers. It reminded him that he had skipped dinner, so he ordered a pulled pork sandwich and a Sprite then sat down in a booth next to a window.

He sat quietly, not opening the file until his food came. Outside, four teenagers, two male and two female, were eating burgers in the bed of a large truck. They were laughing and sharing fries; music was playing from the truck.

It threw him back to when he was a kid—his foster father took him for burgers a couple times a week. They always ate inside, without really saying anything, and Ransom would watch the teenagers in the place having fun, and he pretended he was part of the group, though they never interacted with him. He'd thought his foster father had taken him on the outings because he cared about him. Later, he learned that his foster mother was an escort and a hooker. His foster father had taken him for burgers just to get him out of the house so he didn't see anything he could report to the Department of Child and Family Services.

"Holy shit!"

He looked up and saw the waitress standing next to him, his plate in her hand. He looked down and saw that he had opened the file to a page exposing a photo of a woman in a bed, torn nearly in half by her attacker's blade. It was from a case Jon Stanton had closed several years ago.

"Sorry," he said, hurriedly closing the file.

With a disgusted grunt, she threw his food down on the table, then left. Ransom opened his mouth to say something but changed his mind.

He took a bite of his sandwich. Then he pushed the plate aside and looked around, making sure no one else was near, before he opened the file. He wondered how he had opened it before without noticing.

He skimmed through Stanton's life and mental health record. He noticed Stanton's undergraduate degree in psychology and his master's in neuroscience, then glanced at his doctoral work in psychology. His doctoral thesis had been titled *The Genetics of Sexual Perversion: Predisposition to Evil*. Ransom made a quick note to read the thesis, then moved on to the section he was looking for: Stanton's associations.

He was reportedly still close to his ex-wife. The divorce had been finalized several years ago, and their joint custody of their children gave him visitation every other weekend. The ex-wife made a decent living in real estate and as a personal trainer. The report mentioned no close friends. Ransom re-read that line.

How is it a thirty-four-year-old detective has absolutely no friends? Granted, these investigations were performed by IAD rookies, who occasionally missed things, but that seemed like a mistake that should've been caught.

In the "current relationships" section, there was one name: Sandra Porter.

Ransom knew her well. She was a detective with Vice, and a damn good one from what he had heard. But cases had come across his desk all too frequently with her name on them—everything from excessive force in effectuating an arrest, missing cash after a drug bust, to drug use while undercover. He never had enough evidence to make anything stick; she was too smart for that. It was one of those situations where Ransom had to be patient and wait for the break he was looking for. But he didn't have the time for that.

Today, he was going to make that break himself. He called Rodney Kloves and told him to meet him at an address not far from where he was.

"One more thing, Rodney. I need you to bring something for me from the evidence lockers."

"What's that, boss?"

"Cocaine. Bring a bag of it with you. Just enough for personal use."

"Um..."

"It's for a case."

"I'm still not sure we—"

"You're either with me, or you're against me, Rodney. Which is it?"

There was a pause before he replied, "With you."

"Good. Grab just one bag of coke. Don't get your prints on it. Just bring it here, and we'll have it back in the evidence lockers by morning."

"If you say so."

Ransom hung up. His foster father had taught him to always be the first to hang up. The person to hang up first has the control. He tucked his phone away and pulled his plate closer. A smile parted his lips as he took a bite of the sandwich and stared at the photo of Stanton in the file.

Got you, cocksucker.

20

Calvin Riley parked in front of Taylor's Drugs. Though most stores had their groceries together with the photo development and pharmacy, the pharmacy and photo booth at Taylor's were in a separate building next door.

When he got to the employee break area, he put on his white smock and nametag then went out to the photo booth. Calvin clocked in and counted out the register. During his previous shift, he hadn't been able to get to the stack of undeveloped disposable cameras in the back, and he figured he should finish those first.

Karen stepped out from back and smiled until she saw his face. "Holy shit, Calvin! What happened?"

He turned his face away from her. "Nothing."

She moved closer to him, stopping inches away. Calvin could feel her breath on his neck.

"Oh my hell. Did you go to the hospital?"

"It's nothing. It's mat burn. We were wrestling and my face scraped against the mats."

"Mats did that? No way."

"A lot of guys get it sometimes. It's no big deal."

She looked the wound over and shook her head. "I'm getting Marty. I want him to look at this."

"No," he said too loudly, startling her. "I mean, no. It's fine. Really, I'm fine."

"If you say so." She went around the counter and began to pick up the candy bars that children had pulled off the display. "So what're you doin' this weekend?"

"Nothing. What are you doing?"

"You know Jack? He's having a party. You should come."

"Yeah, he invited me. Then he asked me to bring some pot."

"I got the hook-up on that. Some Hawaiian dude who has it shipped in. Primo stuff. Why don't we pick it up together and head over there?"

He felt something then, a tingling in his belly, but couldn't identify what it was. Excitement maybe? He didn't know. For most of his life, he had felt nothing but a dull numbness to the world around him.

"Cool."

She grinned. "All right, cool."

Calvin spent most of the day in the darkroom, developing photos. The process of developing photos wasn't like it had been a short while ago, at least from what he had read. He knew that even thirty years ago, each individual photo had been developed and looked over, examined to make sure it was sufficient to satisfy the customer. People had taken pride in the job then, and they understood they were doing something important: taking care of people's memories. If the photo processors did their jobs poorly, those memories would be wiped away forever.

Now, a machine developed the photos en masse, and the photo booth employees rarely saw what was on them. But he was different. Even if no one else did, he took pride in his work and looked at each photo to ensure the customers did not receive any imperfections. It took enormous amounts of time, and several shifts a week, he stayed late without pay to catch up on his other work. People said it didn't matter, that the photo industry was almost dead because of cell phones, but he didn't care. He liked the process of being in the dark and looking through people's intimate moments.

Around eight o'clock, he went to the employee break room

and changed. He looked at himself in the mirror over a sink and turned on the water. He let the warm water run over his fingers before applying it to his hair. People had told him he looked like Ethan Hawke, but he never saw it. He had always thought of himself as ugly and asymmetrical. Symmetry was important. People with more symmetrical faces had sex sooner in life, had more partners, were married sooner, and were loved sooner. They had better lives. When he had the money, he was going to get surgery that would make him symmetrical, that would make him perfect.

He headed out to his car, and it started on the first try. When he pulled out onto the street, the sun was gone and night had overtaken the city. San Diego was an odd place. Any family in the world would be lucky to raise their children here. But at the same time, a dark current ran through the streets, where people could be shot for nothing more than giving someone the wrong look.

Like any major city in the world, there was degradation here, and it was like a palpable energy. Calvin could feel it as he drove through the streets, and it lifted anyone who knew what they were looking for: raw humanity, unfiltered by tradition, morals, or conscience.

When Calvin pulled up to Karen Jensen's apartment, he texted her, saying he had arrived. He waited almost five minutes before noticing the group of teenagers staring at him from across the street. He smiled, but one of them held out his arms wide, challenging him to a fight. Calvin thought he looked like a silly bird trying to protect his domain, and he laughed.

The youngster ran over.

"What the fuck you laughin' at, son?" Though only sixteen or seventeen, he was big, and Calvin saw the bulge of the handgun down his pants. He jumped out of the car and stepped toward the boy.

That display was enough. The boy stopped for a second, probably confused as to why Calvin wasn't afraid. But he looked back at his friends, who were shouting at him to kick Calvin's ass, and Calvin knew the boy couldn't back down.

The boy ran up to within a few feet of Calvin and held up his shirt, showing him the handle to what appeared to be an old 9mm. Too quickly for the boy to react, Calvin leapt forward and grabbed the handle of the firearm. He spun around to point the barrel straight at the boy's throat. The boy's eyes reacted only with surprise, not fear, and Calvin knew the gun wasn't loaded.

"Coming at me with an unloaded weapon is a good way to get killed." Calvin dropped the firearm and reached for the FN Five Seven tucked into his own waistband. He brought the weapon up to the boy's head. "This gun and the ammo I got inside it are meant to fire through layers of Kevlar. What do you think it would do to your throat?"

The boy swallowed and looked back at his friends, who were staring blankly at the scene. They looked at each other then broke into a run.

Calvin heard the door to the apartment building behind him open, and he quickly tucked the gun away. "Get outta here."

The boy ran off as Karen stepped out.

"What was that about?" she asked as she climbed into the passenger seat of the Volkswagen.

"Nothing." Calvin got in and pulled away from the curb.

He drove for a few minutes, with Karen flipping through the radio stations before finding a rock station she liked. She sang along with the song as she pulled down the mirror on the sun visor and took out makeup from a small bag in her purse.

"So you still living with your mom?" she said, applying her lipstick.

"Yeah."

"I hated living with my parents. Go left here."

"I have two little brothers. I don't think I could leave them alone. Did you get the pot?"

"Nah, we gotta pick it up. Turn right at the next light. So what's it like living with your mom? Is it weird?"

"No, I love my mom."

She laughed.

"What's so funny?"

"I don't know. It's just weird to hear someone say that out loud. I guess everybody does. It's just weird."

"I don't think it's weird."

"Trust me, Cal—it's weird. It's right up there, next to that gas station."

He stopped the car in front of a dilapidated building with a *For Sale* sign up in the window. The front entrance was boarded up, but two Hispanic males stood in front, smoking. One of them said something to the other then glanced down both sides of the street before coming up to the Beetle.

"What's up, homie? Whatchyu need?"

"Three ounces," Karen said, pulling cash from her purse. She handed it to the man, who counted it and stuffed it into his pocket.

"Be back."

They waited in the car, and Calvin stared forward. He knew a few wrong looks could start a fight. Not that he was frightened; he never was. But he had noticed that the two other Hispanic males across the street had come up behind the car.

"You always buy your pot here?"

"Yeah, don't let 'em scare you. They're cool. They're businessmen."

"They don't look like businessmen."

"They fuck me over, and I go back and tell all my friends. They tell all their friends, and they tell all their friends, and these guys are outta business. They know that. They won't fuck with us. Just relax."

After a few minutes, another male came up to the car. He was no more than fourteen or fifteen years old, but already had the tattoos on the neck and fingers marking him for life.

He handed Calvin the weed and ran back to the alley between the gas station and the building. Calvin was about to pull away when something on the second floor of the house caught his eye. A white male in a black-collared shirt was speaking into a phone. Maybe in his forties, he had curly hair and a soft, almost boyish face.

"Fuck," Calvin shouted, his tires screeching as he sped away.

As the momentum threw Karen back into the seat, she bumped her head against the headrest. "Calvin, what the fuck!"

"They're cops."

"What?"

The sound of sirens closed in behind them as two cruisers pulled out of thin air. One was on the east side of the street, and one on the west. The cruisers came up behind the Beetle, their sirens blaring, as Calvin cut off a Ford and swung the car around onto the opposite side of the street.

"Calvin! Stop!"

He pushed the pedal as far as it would go and got up to seventy miles per hour before the cruisers had even turned around. In front of them, two of the cops, the males who had been standing in front of the door, were waiting in the middle of the road, their guns drawn.

"Duck," he said calmly.

"What! What the fuck! Stop!"

He lowered his head to the top of the steering wheel so they couldn't get a good shot, and he edged the car over to the center of the road. The cops shouted at him to stop, then the high-pitched ting of slugs hitting his car echoed in his ears, and he laughed.

The car sped between the two cops as they jumped out of the way to avoid getting hit. Calvin sat up, despite the cops firing from behind him, and turned down a residential street. The cruisers weren't anywhere near him, and he spotted an open garage with a truck in it. He pulled in next to the truck and waited.

"What the fuck!"

"You say that too much," he said, pulling out a package of gum and taking a stick.

"It's like a two-hundred-dollar fine. Why would you do that?" she said, punching him in the arm.

He laughed and popped the gum into his mouth. "It was fun. Nobody got hurt."

She punched him again. "You're such an asshole."

"Relax, we're fine. Nothing's gonna happen."

"Well, what are we supposed to do now? We're in someone's garage."

Calvin rolled down his window and heard voices coming from the backyard. "They're busy. We're cool for a minute." He saw the control panel for the garage door and got out to close the door.

It was slow going down, and the sounds of sirens grew louder. As the door touched the cement floor, three cruisers shot past. Calvin went to the small windows on the doors and looked out.

"What if they find us here?" Karen asked.

"Then they find us. No big deal." He looked at the door leading into the house. "Let's go see what's inside."

"Are you crazy? I'm not going into someone's house."

"Stay here then."

"Calvin, where are you going? Calvin!"

He tried the knob. It turned, and he opened the door and stepped inside. The house was quiet except for music and voices in the back. He went to the sliding-glass door and looked out at the backyard. Several people were mingling in front of tiki torches with drinks in their hands, and Jimmy Buffett was playing over outdoor speakers.

He stepped away from the doors and into the kitchen. The large stainless-steel fridge had French doors. It was full of food, and he sifted through until he found a bottle of beer. He popped it open then swallowed half the bottle in a few gulps. He opened a Styrofoam container and found some old spaghetti with meat sauce and a roll. He took it out and was walking to the microwave when he noticed the small pair of eyes watching him from the hallway.

A young girl stood there, staring at him. He placed the food down on the counter. "Hi," he said.

"Hi."

"Do you know who I am?"

"No."

"I'm your uncle."

"No, you're not."

"Sure, I am. I can prove it. What's your name?"

"Jennifer."

"See, I knew that. That's what I was going to say. That your name was Jennifer."

She smiled, and he smiled back and walked toward her.

He leaned down. "Are those your parents in the backyard?"

"Yeah."

"Well I think—"

"Calvin," Karen shouted in a whisper, "get your ass out here, and let's go."

He turned away from the young girl and took a large handful of the spaghetti, shoving it into his mouth as he headed for the garage. He opened the garage door on his way to the car. When he pulled out, the street was quiet, so he turned back to the main road and blended in with the congested traffic of rush hour.

21

Ransom awoke in the driver's seat of his car. On the passenger seat was a small baggie of coke covered by the Stanton file. Sandra hadn't come home the night before, and he'd told Rodney to call it a night. But he'd decided to stay. He sat up, checking his watch as he leaned his head back against the headrest. He closed his eyes, swearing it was just to rest, but quickly fell into a dreamless sleep.

Ransom jolted awake to the sound of a powerful engine roaring up the street and coming to a stop in front of Sandra Porter's house. Disheveled, Sandra stepped out of the car, a cigarette dangling from her mouth. She looked like the girlfriend of a strung-out rock star.

After she climbed the steps and went inside her house, Ransom waited half a minute then stuffed the coke in his pocket and got out. He knocked on her front door and waited what seemed like a long time before she answered.

"What the hell do you want?" she asked.

"Can I come in?"

"Do I have a choice?"

"No."

She left the door open as she went back inside and collapsed onto the couch, her hand over her eyes to keep out the light. Ransom went over to her and sat on the end of the couch near her feet. He noticed that she had on high heels and reeked of cigarette smoke and sex.

"Who'd you fuck last night?"

"None of your damn business, Ransom. What the hell do you

want anyway? I got a shift in a few hours."

"No, you don't. You're on administrative leave, pending an Internal Affairs investigation."

"I didn't do anything."

He pulled out the baggie of coke and held it up.

Her eyes went to it then to him. "You're a fucking—"

"Might want to be careful what you say just now. It's part of the official questioning that's going into the report."

She didn't respond, and he couldn't suppress the smirk that came to his lips.

He scooted over on the couch and put her heels up on his lap, removed them, and began to massage her feet. "I don't give a shit about busting you with coke. What it does, though, is gimme probable cause to call out some uniforms and search your house. What they gonna find here, Sandy?"

"I've never done anything to you. Why are you fucking with me?"

"Because I want something from you."

"What?"

"Your boyfriend."

She said nothing, so he took a deep breath and leaned back on the couch, enjoying the quiet of the house.

"I know your father. We're not friends or anything, but I know him. We've met at a couple of political functions. He told me about you. Said that he got you into Harvard. It's amazing what money can do, isn't it? A straight-D student getting into Harvard 'cause her daddy made a couple of calls? So I thought, 'Why would she turn that down and choose to be a cop?' Hell, you could probably just lay around the beach all day and have Daddy take care of you, so why would you bust your ass as a cop for six years? Do you even know why you did what you did?"

"I wanted to make a difference."

"Bullshit. You would'a joined the Peace Corps or Green Peace or some other hippie organization. Becoming a cop wasn't your style. You're afraid. That's why you did it. You're afraid that the world just pushes you around. Little Sandra Porter had no power over her life. But now you do. That gun and that badge give you power, don't they? Helluva rush the first time you pull that gun out and see the look of terror in the piece'a shit's eyes that you had to draw it on. I got an erection the first time. Was it arousing for you?"

"Get out of my house."

He shrugged. "If that's what you want. But I'll just be waiting out there and calling in the warrant. Shouldn't take more than a few minutes for me to email a judge, asking for an e-warrant, and maybe ten minutes after that to get all the uniforms here. Can you flush everything you have in this house that quickly?" He placed his hand over hers. "Are there things here that won't flush?"

She closed her eyes as if to say a prayer. Then she opened them again, refusing to look at him. "He's a good cop. You won't find anything."

"Leave that to me. And if you're telling the truth, that's good, too. I just want to know for sure—that's all. I'm not looking to lock him up if he hasn't done anything. But Harlow and that whole mess—that's gotta end. Jon's one of Harlow's, like our new assistant chief, but I heard through the grapevine he's moving back to San Francisco. That leaves Jon as the last man on the force to be one of Harlow's guys."

"If he's clean, will you leave him alone?"

"Absolutely. I'm not looking to bust good cops. We got few enough of them in this city as it is."

She dragged her feet away and rose. She went to the kitchen and pulled a cigarette from a pack then lit it with a lighter she got from a drawer. Leaning over the counter, she tipped her ashes into the sink and watched the small particles of gray fade and disappear on the wet surface.

"What do you want me to do?"

22

Stanton awoke at three in the morning with a severe migraine. His vision was blurry, and colors appeared in the darkness around him. He stumbled out of bed and took several prescription ibuprofen, swallowing them without water. He went to urinate then drank a few handfuls of water out of the faucet before going back to bed.

Unable to sleep, he just lay there, staring at the ceiling. Moonlight shining through the blinds created slits of light up his walls, and he watched them so long that the moonlight turned to sunlight. Then his alarm went off.

Stanton pounded the alarm with a fist as he did nearly every morning, promising himself that he wasn't going to use alarms any longer. Something about the jarring sound, especially when he was still asleep, sent waves of pain through his skull. He knew it was his imagination, but the pain seemed so real that he broke a new clock every month or so.

He took his juice and a breakfast bar to the balcony. He watched the surfers sitting idle out on the sea, waiting for any wave that would propel them back to shore, but none came. Eventually, they gave up and paddled back to lie on the beach a while longer and see if anybody else caught any waves.

Stanton's phone rang. It was Assistant Chief Ho.

"Hey, Chin."

"Morning. Not a bad time, I hope?"

"No, just finishing breakfast. What's going on?"

"The suit's been filed by the Putnam family, Jon. It's not good. It's a wrongful death suit blaming you for Putnam's death."

"That's what I figured."

"They're asking for twenty-six million dollars."

"We guessed it was going to be high."

"Not that high. They haven't talked settlement yet, but word is they want at least two mil to make this go away. The county doesn't have two mil to spare right now, Jon. We need to win this thing."

"I understand. What do you need from me?"

"We're hiring outside counsel for this. It's a law firm downtown. Stoll, Cran & Wilson."

"I know them."

"How?"

"They were Melissa's attorneys during the divorce."

"Oh. They didn't mention anything about that. Do you think that's going to be a problem?"

"Not for me. They're good."

"Okay, well, we'll deal with it later, I guess. Meet them as soon as you can. Ask for Taylor Rowe."

"It's Saturday. I've got the kids."

"Sorry, Jon. They're making a special meeting just for you today to get things up and running. Can you pick up your kids after?"

"I guess. I've got one thing to follow up on this morning and then I'll head down. Thanks, Chin."

"You're welcome. Just get this going. Their lawyer's a real asshole with connections. So the faster this is over with, the better."

Stanton ended the call and looked out over the sea, stretching his neck, still feeling a slight burn as the skin pulled over the wound on his back. He called Melissa and the boys to tell them he would have to pick them up later for their day at the zoo.

Stanton changed into a wetsuit. While his shirt was off, he studied the scar beginning to develop over the wound. It looped around his ribs and hooked up to the middle of his back. He had a lot of scars, and each was a reminder, telling him he had lived and had survived.

Stanton went down to the beach with his board and paddled out about fifty feet. He turned back to shore and watched the people on the beach. A few of the girls were topless, and a group of men leered at them from a dozen yards away.

He turned over on his back and stared up at the sky, squinting against the bright sunlight. There were no clouds, just an endless landscape of sky. A plane streaked across, leaving a trail of gray smoke through the perfect blue, and it reminded him of his scar, except the contrail would slowly fade to nothing.

He lay on the water as long as he could, but once he started shivering, he headed back to shore. The men were still staring at the girls, guzzling beers to build up their courage, and Stanton walked by them on the way to his apartment.

"They're sixteen," he said. "Touch them, and you'll all go to prison."

As Stanton walked away, one of the men shouted, "It'd be worth it."

After a quick shower and a change of clothing, he headed downtown to the law offices of Stoll, Cran & Wilson. They were in the Advanced Equities Plaza building, and Stanton parked curbside rather than going into the building parking garage. The building was twenty-three stories of dark glass and precisely cut steel carving out space at sharp angles. Its post-modern style was meant to give viewers the sense that the building jutted from the ground naturally, like a mountain of steel and glass.

Inside, the floor gleamed from a recent mopping. The artificial lighting was minimal as most of the glass walls allowed natural light to pour in, filling the entire lobby with a warm glow. A security guard sitting behind a large desk looked up at Stanton as he approached.

"Hi," Stanton said. "I'm here for Stoll, Cran & Wilson."

"Twenty-first floor on your left."

Stanton took the elevator up, and it came to an abrupt stop near the top of the building. He stepped off into the law firm's plush lobby. A young girl sat at the receptionist desk on her cell phone.

Stanton told her who he was.

"Taylor will be out in a sec. Do you want anything to drink?"

"Diet Coke would be fine."

"Sure." She walked to a vending machine down one of the hallways and input a code then returned with a Diet Coke.

"Thanks."

"Sure thing."

"So do you guys always work Saturdays?"

"Nope. We're actually here just for you."

"Sorry about that. It wasn't my choice."

"No worries."

Stanton flipped through one of the *Time* magazines on the coffee table, and a few minutes later, Taylor Rowe walked out. She was slender, with muscular legs wrapped in a tight red skirt. She wore a white blouse with a silver bracelet and necklace to match, and her hair was pinned up in the back.

"Detective Stanton." She held out her hand. "Taylor Rowe."

"Nice to meet you," he said, standing to shake her hand.

"You seem surprised."

"No, I had been given the impression you were male. Sorry, that was dumb."

"My father actually was convinced I was a boy, and he wanted to name me Taylor. When I was born, the name had grown on them too much to abandon."

He returned her slight smile, appreciating the minor revelation she had felt comfortable enough to share.

"Come on back to my office, Detective."

He followed her through the hallways, admiring the abstract art. The interior walls were a deep gray, and all the art was red, white, or black. He paused at a particular piece for a few moments. A man stood upright in a room, surrounded by black. It was meant, no doubt, to be a man in an office, but that wasn't how it came across.

"Interesting piece," he said.

"Our senior partners pick all the art. Well, one of them anyway. He's really into the abstract thing. Travels all over the world to find them. I think we got that one in Moscow. Just up here on the right, Detective."

Her spacious office had leather furniture and floor-to-ceiling windows that looked out over the city. She sat down and put her feet up on a small leather footstool behind her desk, and Stanton sat across from her. She had no decorations or photos anywhere. The only things marking the office as hers were her degrees hung by the door.

"I heard you have a PhD in psychology," she said. "Impressive for a cop... sorry, that came out wrong. It's impressive for anybody. Just unexpected in a cop."

"I suppose the same could be said for a lawyer with an undergraduate degree in dance."

She smiled. "I wasn't even going to hang that up, but I thought it would be weird to just have a law degree."

"What made you give up dance?"

"Reality and the thought of not being able to eat. No money in dance."

"If you really loved it, you wouldn't have cared."

She shifted uncomfortably in her seat, and Stanton knew he had inadvertently hit a nerve. He usually controlled that impulse, but occasionally, he let his guard drop and pressed the shatter-point in someone's psyche, which that person denied even—or maybe especially—to themselves.

"Sorry, I shouldn't have said that."

"No, your perception's accurate. I thought I did love it. I followed it all my life and then gave it up because I thought that maybe it'd be too hard. It's not something I talk about very frequently." She opened a file on her desktop. "Let's talk about you, though. You know what the suit is and what they're looking for, right?"

"Yes."

"Good. It's a straightforward case. The complaint alleges negligence, but that's not what Coop is going for. That's not his style. If we ever do get to a trial, he's going to make it seem like you purposely pushed Putnam off that building."

"The Crime Scene Unit and the ME's Office cleared me and said there was no evidence to suggest that."

"He fell from too high to really have much left to analyze."

"When people are thrown or pushed from a building, they go farther out because of the momentum. When they jump, they usually fall closer to the building. Darrell landed seven feet from the building's entrance; far too close to have been thrown."

"That may be so, but Coop will try his best to paint you as a psycho cop who's finally taken the law into his own hands. It's what he does. A lot of juries buy it. The general public doesn't really know what it's like to be a cop, and they expect you to be perfect all the time. It's a tough presumption to overcome. One drunk and disorderly ticket, too many divorces, missing some child support payments, and the jury thinks you're not fit to wear that uniform." She bit the tip of her pen. "But Putnam was about as horrible a person as you could find. I think Coop's overplaying his hand on this. He's got his defense attorney glasses on and doesn't realize how much the public really hates child molesters."

"What would you like from me?"

"We need to go into your history, particularly your disciplinary record—any drug use, sexual perversions you've shared with other people, stuff like that. We also have some interrogatories that I just sent general denials on. The next step is going to be to schedule a deposition in a month or so."

"That fast?"

"Knowing Coop, he's going to want to capitalize on the publicity this case has already gotten. He'll try to move this along to trial as fast as possible." She opened a Word document that held a long list of questions then pulled the keyboard near her. "So let's begin."

Stanton answered questions in Rowe's office for nearly four hours. They took no breaks, and miraculously, it didn't seem to affect Rowe at all, but by the end, Stanton's head was throbbing from an impending migraine. Lately, he'd been feeling the sting of age for the first time in his life.

"Are we almost done?" he asked.

"Do you want to be done?"

"I wouldn't mind. I'm supposed to take my kids to the zoo."

"We can stop here, I guess. But at some point, you're going to have to come in and finish, and then we need to begin the preparations for the deposition."

"Sure. I'll come by during the week some time."

"Fridays work best. There's usually no court appearances."

He rose. "I appreciate your help in this."

"My pleasure. My mom was a cop. I volunteered for this case, actually. I probably shouldn't tell you this, but I followed that stuff in the papers with you and Eli Sherman and Chief Harlow. Intriguing stuff."

"Opinions vary I guess."

As he was leaving, Rowe said, "Jon? Stay out of trouble in the meantime."

He grinned. "I'll try."

23

The trip to the zoo was hurried, but the boys enjoyed it. Stanton took them directly to the big cat exhibit, and from there, they explored the rest of the zoo before going out for pizza and heading home. They were supposed to spend the night, but Melissa was going to visit her parents in Napa and wanted them back because they had an early flight Sunday morning. When he dropped them off, they ran to their mother's arms after hugging and kissing Stanton. Melissa waved from the porch but didn't go over.

Afterward, he felt relaxed, as he always did after spending time with his family. Though the beach was calling to him, he felt he had something else to do. It was already getting dark, but he drove to the Adams' home and parked up the street about twenty feet, just far enough away that he could see into the house without their noticing him.

Stanton listened to a jazz station on the radio, and after twenty minutes, an old silver Mustang pulled into the Adams' driveway. A man in khakis and a plaid button-down stepped out, then got his two daughters out of the back. They were close in age, and Stanton couldn't tell which was Tracey.

The man teased the girls about something and pinned one of them against the car to tickle her. Laughing, the other one ran up from behind and jumped on his back. The man feigned a heart attack and fell over onto the hood of the car. When they had stopped laughing, the girls went into the house as the man took out a rag and began wiping down a few places on the car.

Stanton flipped through Sarah's file and found the photos

her parents had given him. A few were recent, but he stared at the second grade picture of her smiling widely with a missing front tooth. He got out of the car.

"Hi," he said, walking up to Tracey's father.

"Can I help you with something?"

Stanton resisted the urge to pull out his badge. "I'm Jon Stanton with the San Diego PD."

"Oh, you're the cop. Yeah, my wife told me about you. I think she already told you to—"

"Talk to your lawyer, I know. I'm very familiar with your lawyer already." He turned to the car. "Sixty-eight?"

"Sixty-seven."

Stanton whistled. "My grandfather used to work on old muscle cars in the summer when I went to their ranch. He used to let me drive around a sixty-nine COPO Chevelle."

"You're kidding me? I would give my arm for a COPO Chevelle. They only made around three hundred of 'em."

"I know that now. He offered me either that or a horse for my sixteenth birthday, and I chose the horse."

"Holy shit." He chuckled. "That sucks."

"What can you do?" Stanton paused a moment, admiring the car. "What's your name?"

"Robert. You can call me Bob."

"Bob, I know what you guys are worried about. If Tracey was my daughter, I'd be worried, too. But I promise you I am not interested in getting her into any trouble. I just want to find who killed Sarah."

"Killed? I thought she was just missing?"

"She is. I'm sorry. I should be more careful with my words. She is just missing. But she's been missing a long time, and we haven't found a trace of evidence relating to her disappearance. The likelihood of her being alive is almost non-existent. For all intents and purposes, I have to treat this like a homicide."

Bob shook his head and leaned against the car. "Damn shame. She was a nice girl."

Stanton pulled out the photo and a pen and wrote his number on the back of the picture. "Please just hang on to this. I know you don't want me to talk to Tracey, but if you ever get the chance, if you could ask her if she knows anything about Sarah's disappearance, I would consider it a personal favor. And I remember all my favors."

Bob took the photo and paused just a second too long before lowering it.

I've got you, Stanton thought.

"Can't do it, Detective. I'm sorry. My wife would kill me."

"I understand." He began backing up, staring at the car. "Love the car. Take care of it, it'll be one of a kind one day."

Stanton went to his car without looking back. He had hit the wrong target inadvertently. The mother was, in all likelihood, the one allowing the sex parties, and Bob might not even know about them. Stanton doubted he would stick around once he found out. The love he showed for his daughters was genuine, and he guessed the mother was actually a stepmother. He liked Bob and wished he could turn around and tell him right away what was going on, but Bob wouldn't believe him. People's potential to be willfully blind was amazing.

Stanton started his car and drove up the street past the Adams' house. He saw Bob still standing by the Mustang, staring at the photo in his hand.

24

The next day, Stanton woke up early and went surfing. The slow, rolling waves allowed him to think and meditate rather than focus on his actions. The water was cold from a coming storm farther out to sea, but the sun was bright, and plenty of people were around.

Stanton struck up a conversation with a woman on the beach who had asked him where he learned to surf, and he described the lessons his mother had put him in when he was young. She asked if he would be willing to teach her, and he politely declined. There was something about surfing and its lessons that he kept completely to himself. He wasn't selfish in many areas, but surfing was one thing he shared with few people.

Afterward, he went to church at his local ward for half an hour before a migraine forced him to cut church early.

As he was leaving after service, Stanton found a small silver lighter in the parking lot. He took it back to the lost and found, and the clerk, an elderly woman with thick glasses, inspected its intricate engravings then said, "Keep it."

He thought about throwing it away, but the engravings were so detailed that he felt like it would be a shame, so he stuck it in his pocket.

Stanton drove to Melissa's house to see the boys then remembered she was out of town. So instead, he drove home and decided to read out on his balcony.

By the time he looked up from his book, it was getting dark, and traffic on the street below was dying down. He stretched and stood up, feeling the breeze hit his face as he watched the waves roll into shore. A few bonfires went up on the beach.

He went inside and looked at the television, but decided he was too tired to watch it. He went to bed, but something was keeping him up and tying his stomach in knots, and he couldn't tell what it was. Before he could figure it out, he drifted off to sleep.

The sound of his cell phone jarred Stanton awake. His eyes adjusting to the darkness and the dim light of the moon coming through the windows, he turned to his nightstand and answered the call. "Hello?"

"Jon. I'm sorry to wake you. This is Bob. Um, Adams, from yesterday."

"I remember. What's going on, Bob?"

"I talked to Tracey." Bob was whispering, and the sound had a slight echo. Stanton guessed he was in a bathroom. "She told me that Sarah had been hanging out with some guy nobody else knew. She said he was older, but she doesn't know how much older. I asked who this guy was, but she didn't know. She did say he would come by the school every Wednesday and walk Sarah home. He worked Wednesdays nearby, I guess."

Stanton frantically wrote everything down on the notepad app on his iPad. He repeated, "Wednesdays at school, probably worked nearby" to himself until he finally got it down into the document and hit the save button.

"Was there anything else she told you, Bob?"

"Not really. Just that the guy was pretty good looking and young."

"I really appreciate this. I promise it'll stay between us."

"Thanks." He hesitated. "And, Detective, if you catch the bastard, you don't let him get away with it. You hear me?"

"I do. Thanks again."

"No problem."

After he hung up, Stanton was too excited to sleep again. Instead of fighting it, he went out on the balcony in his T-shirt and boxer shorts and researched Sarah's school and businesses within a mile radius of it. Then he re-read the file for anything he had missed.

The sun came up a few hours later, but he didn't notice.

25

Monday morning at the San Diego Police Northern Division was about as busy as it got. Drunks and meth-heads who had been locked in the tank over the weekend were being released, and detectives were assigned new cases at the morning briefing.

Stanton sat in the back row next to a detective whom everyone referred to as Slim Jim because he was a hundred fifty-eight pounds and six feet one. He was dressed in a rumpled gray suit and reeked of alcohol. He stirred sugar and milk into his coffee then burped before taking a sip.

"Hate these fucking things," Slim Jim said. "In Hollywood, they upload new cases for you in your drop box, and you meet with the brass when you want to."

"I heard they also do a lot of cocaine from the evidence lockers. That true?"

He shrugged.

Childs was at the front of the room, talking about a drug bust the precinct narcs unit was handling with the DEA. It was a meth lab consisting of four homes on the same block. A single person had bought all the homes, and only one of them was supposed to contain the labs. The other three were cover so the lab would have no neighbors.

"You believe that shit?" Slim Jim said. "I'd blow a horse for half a house in that neighborhood, and some tweeker's got four of 'em."

"Not for long."

"Gentlemen," Childs said, looking at them, "something you'd like to share with the class?"

"No, sir," Slim Jim said.

"Good. Then keep your mouths shut and listen up. You may not be risking your ass on this raid, but some of us are, so show some damned respect."

"Sorry, sir."

The meeting continued for another half hour and concluded with Childs asking Stanton to stay a little while afterward. As the other officers filed out, he came to the front of the room and pulled up a chair while Childs finished closing windows on his laptop and turned off the projector.

"Heard you're workin' the Putnam disappearances again."

"Where'd you hear that?"

"Is it important?"

"I'd like to know."

"School cop at the Huntington Academy called me. He wanted me to make sure that you knew you didn't hear anything from him."

"Danny, I'm close. I've got something right now that wasn't in the initial investigation. I need to follow up on it."

"We're getting our asses sued right now. You should'a told me you was doin' this. It's gotta stop."

"I just need another couple of weeks. I can even do it on my own time."

"No deal. Some piece'a shit reporter finds out you're still investigating, and the papers the next day say we think Putnam's innocent and we killed the wrong man."

"I didn't kill him."

"To the public, you may as well have." He closed his laptop and put it in his bag before slinging it over his shoulder. "I'm serious about this. It comes straight from the chief. No more investigating that shit."

"What if we were wrong?" Stanton asked as Childs was nearly out the door. "What if we chased the wrong guy, and the one who took those girls is still out there?"

"Then Lord forgive us, Jon. But until then, leave the fucking cases alone."

Stanton drove by Woodrow Wilson Elementary and felt a tug of guilt as he parked his car across the street. This was the last place on earth anyone had seen Sarah alive. Childs had given him a direct order, and disobeying that order was enough to stick him with desk duty. Meeting with the crazies who inevitably came into the station wanting to file complaints against aliens for robbing them, the CIA for sending them messages, or their neighbors for being members of the KGB. Childs might even suspend him without pay, just to teach him a lesson. Childs was from a military background, and he didn't tolerate flagrant disobedience.

Stanton waited around through recess, left for lunch, and returned to wait another two and a half hours before school let out for the day. He had received twenty emails during that time, and he attempted to return each of them. As the kids filed out, he put away his phone.

He scanned the perimeter of the school and the edges of the fence and the parking lot. The person he was looking for wouldn't stand out. He wouldn't have tattoos over his face and neck. He wouldn't have piercings covering his face or a gun protruding from underneath his shirt. He would appear normal, almost inconspicuous. And after his arrest, everyone who knew him would be shocked that he could have committed such monstrous crimes. Everyone except the people who really knew him—his mother and his wife. They might be willfully blind, but somewhere, swimming in the middle of all the denial and self-loathing, they had accepted that something was wrong with him. Of course, they would never tell a living soul about their concerns until it was too late.

After the standard crowd of parents had gone, no one stuck around. No one was waiting near the fences, watching from the periphery, or just happening to walk by on the sidewalk. As soon as the kids had cleared out, Stanton started his car and left.

He would come back on Wednesday.

26

Calvin Riley finished his shift and sat in his car for over an hour, debating whether to go home. His mother had given him a strict command: be home by seven for dinner or go to bed without it. He knew what that meant. For his mother, not eating dinner that she had prepared was a personal insult.

He remembered how suffocated he'd felt at home when he was younger. School had bored him immensely, so the only place he'd felt at ease was by himself on the streets. San Diego had some extraordinarily pleasant neighborhoods, and Calvin would walk through them, staring at the large mansions and dreaming of one day living on his own in one of them. He imagined having a wife, and they would have friends over—friends who were interested in what he had to say. And then after the friends had left, he and his wife would have sex in their hot tub and watch television in bed until they fell asleep in each other's arms.

But that wasn't how it had worked out. The weight of reality had fallen on him, and he realized he would never have that life. He couldn't even if he tried. His mother would never let him. She would never leave him alone.

He decided he didn't feel like going home, but there was someplace else he did feel like going. He started the car and drove to the freeway. Within twenty minutes, he had pulled onto Cotton Drive, where he parked on the curb in front of a three-story red-brick house. A Mercedes was parked there now, and Calvin knew that Brian Underwood preferred to park there when he got home late, rather than in the five-car garage.

Calvin looked into all the windows, starting from the top and working his way down. There was no activity in most of the rooms, but the lights were on in the kitchen and the basement.

The thought of the basement made him uncomfortable, and he looked away for a minute before turning back to see the family gathering around a massive dinner table. Brian and his wife, Shelly, sat with their two sons, Luke and Lance, and their daughter, Lexi.

Lexi was already sitting at the table, playing on a phone, earbuds in her ears. Her brother Luke ran over, pulled the earbuds off, and tried running away with them. Lexi shouted something and chased after him. Calvin saw them through the living room window. She tackled Luke on the couch and punched him in the kidneys. *Good for her. Don't take shit from anyone.*

Another car pulled up. He hadn't expected any visitors, and it made him nervous. He ducked down, staying up just enough that he could still see, and watched an elderly couple step out of an Escalade. The man held the door open for the woman, then they walked to the door and knocked. The children scurried over to the door and opened it, throwing their arms around the couple. *Grandparents.*

Calvin thought of his own grandparents, Grandpa Norman and his wife, Belle. Calvin's real grandmother had run off before he was born, and no one knew where she was. But Belle had filled the role of grandmother as best she could. She cooked for Norman's family every weekend and took the grandchildren to free activities like farms or parks. Both Norman and Belle had grown up during the Depression, and even the thought of spending money unnecessarily set them off into a lecture about the value of a dollar.

Calvin remembered Grandpa Norman on the couch, watching the football game. He and his brothers had been there because their mother had a job interview; Calvin was in charge of seeing that his little brothers were fed and stayed out of trouble.

Calvin had gone to the closet by the upstairs bedroom and retrieved a rifle. His grandpa had taken him shooting several times, and he knew the feel of the rifle. He also knew the ammunition was locked in a safe in the bedroom. Belle had been asleep in there, so he was quiet as he went to the safe, put in the combo, and retrieved the ammunition. He'd then gone downstairs to find that Grandpa Norman had fallen asleep.

Calvin had lifted the rifle and placed the barrel against his grandfather's head, right at the bald spot. Then he pulled the trigger, spraying blood over the coffee table and the couch. The sound had deafened him, and the recoil had knocked the rifle out of his hands. The television had been spattered in a pulpy mess. He went to it and ran his fingers over the screen, tracing a drawing in his grandfather's pulverized tissue until he heard footsteps coming down the stairs.

He got the rifle just as Belle ran downstairs. As she'd stood frozen in shock, he'd lifted it and fired two rounds, hitting her in the chest twice. Then he'd looked down at her face a long time, watching life leave her. He remembered her eyes had looked like a doll's eyes. How strange that he could see that.

Afterward, he'd made sure his brothers were okay, then called 911 and sat on the patio, waiting for his mother to arrive.

He remembered everyone, from the police and his mother, to the psychiatrists and the judge, asking him only one question: *Why?* The only answer he had ever given seemed the most suitable even now: *Because I wanted to see what would happen.*

A knock on the car window made Calvin jump. He looked over to see a man in a sweat-suit standing there, motioning for Calvin to roll down the window.

"Yeah?" Calvin said.

"You're parked in front of my driveway."

"Oh, oh, hey, I'm sorry. I'm waiting for my girlfriend to get ready. Here, I'll pull up."

He pulled the car up about ten feet and waited for the man to drive away in his red sedan. Calvin looked at the house one more time before heading home.

27

Stanton's phone rang early in the morning, while he was brushing his teeth. He ran to the kitchen to grab it. He spit into the sink before answering.

"Detective, it's Taylor Rowe, your lawyer."

"Oh, hey. What can I do for you?"

"Just got off the phone with Coop. We have our first deposition scheduled for this Wednesday at ten at his office."

"That seems quick."

"It is. Not to intimidate you, Detective, 'cause I don't think it's too big a deal, but Coop used to clerk with the judge we've been assigned."

"You don't think that's a big deal?"

"No, because I know this judge. I think he can be impartial. Just make sure you're there Wednesday. It's not your deposition. In fact, you don't need to worry about it for a while until we fully prep you, but it's good to be there for all of them and hear what everybody else is saying."

"If you think it's important, I'll be there."

"I do. Do you need the address?"

"I'll look it up online. Thanks."

"Call me if you have any questions, Detective."

"You can call me Jon."

Stanton hung up and finished brushing his teeth. He dressed in a blue button-down with a white collar and black pinstripe pants. When he was still married to Melissa, the family gathered nearly every morning in the walk-in closet, and she and the boys would pick out Stanton's clothes for the day. It was a deal they had going: if the boys did their chores without being nagged, Stanton had to wear whatever outfit they chose. There had been more than one incident of Christmas sweater and jeans.

He headed down to the precinct and parked behind the building next to the cruisers. The uniforms standing outside gave him the cold shoulder. He had testified against the former police chief, Harlow, and no matter what their sins, officers were expected to look out for one another. A cop who had testified against one of their own couldn't be trusted.

The building was full of officers, detectives, and staff, and it brought a warm feeling to him. Something about a fully functioning police station, each person doing his or her best... he had seen so much of the opposite—so much corruption and wickedness.

In his office, he sat down a second, going over what he needed to be doing. He played absently with the lighter in his pocket and ran his fingers over the engravings; he had decided they were words in a language he couldn't identify. But he liked the smoothness of the silver and the easy glide of the roller before the flame ignited. Occasionally, he held onto things like napkins or pens and carried them with him to play with when he needed something to occupy his mind.

He'd been neglecting two dozen other cases while following up on Sarah Henroid's disappearance. He opened his computer and went to the first case. A twenty-one-year-old woman had been gang-raped outside a popular bar near La Mesa. Several witnesses had driven or walked by as the assault was occurring, but no one called the police.

Stanton began with the sketch-artist drawings produced from the victim's descriptions of her three assailants. He would interview the witnesses and attempt to get the assailants' names then track them down. But he knew another, possibly quicker, way to identify them. Men who would openly rape a woman in public wouldn't think twice about returning to the same bar. Finding them was just a matter of getting one of the witnesses down there with a couple of undercovers on a Friday or Saturday night until the rapists showed.

"Hey."

Stanton looked up to see Sandra leaning against the doorframe. She was wearing jeans and a sleeveless tight black shirt that exposed her muscular arms.

She sat down across from him. "How's the Putnam thing going?"

"Not good. I was taken off the case."

Sandra hesitated a moment, staring at him with her cobalt eyes. She lifted her shirt, exposing the thin clip and piece of sports tape from the wire.

"Do you wanna grab lunch later?" she asked as she took a pad of paper and a pen off his desk.

"Sure."

She wrote Ransom Talano's name on the notepad. "Should I just swing by here?"

"Yeah. Come by around noon. I have some paperwork to catch up on."

"Okay, I'll see you then."

As she left, Stanton followed her. She went to her office and was in there for about five minutes before stepping out.

"I took it off," she said.

"What's going on?"

"He wants me to help him. He thinks you're still part of that whole Harlow thing."

"And you agreed?"

"I didn't have a choice."

"Why not?"

She glanced away and wouldn't look at him.

"Sandy, why not?"

"He threatened to execute a search warrant on my house."

"So what? Every cop's house gets tossed. That's part of the job."

"He knows things about me, Jon."

"Like what?"

"I don't want to talk about it here. Come to my house tonight."

As she left, Stanton went back to his office and sat in his chair, staring at the ceiling. He had known several cops like Talano; they never stopped coming. No matter what.

For just a moment, he contemplated whether looking into Talano himself would be worth the hassle, then he left his office and headed down to HR. Though many people considered him a snitch, a few still owed him favors.

Connie Penti was at the main HR desk, filling out paperwork when Stanton got there. She was wearing her uniform; her long black hair clipped in the back. Stanton could smell her apple bodywash, along with the distinct odor of vodka and cigarette smoke that the bodywash was meant to cover up.

"Well, well," she said, "look who comes down to pay us a visit."

"How are you, Connie?"

"'Nother day in paradise, you know. How you doin', sweetheart? You holdin' up okay?"

"Good as can be expected I guess. How's Isaac?"

"He's almost done with his electrical engineering degree and should be outta school in another couple months."

"No way? Congrats. That's exciting."

"Hell yes, it is. Then I can quit and get my ass home to take care of my kids."

Stanton pushed a pen away from the edge of the counter then glanced around to make sure no one else was here.

"Uh oh," she said.

"What?"

"Don't 'what' me. I know that look. What do you need?"

"I could never fool you."

"I got six boys, Jonny. You ain't foolin' me 'bout anything."

"Ransom Talano. He's after me for whatever reason, and thinks I'm cut from the same cloth as Harlow. He's gotten Sandra to flip on me."

"Lord help us when we got cops turnin' on cops."

"I just need to know what I'm dealing with, Connie. Nothing hush-hush, just what he's investigating me for and what he wants."

She exhaled loudly and crossed her arms. "We need this job right now, you know."

"I know. And I won't do anything that puts you at risk of losing it."

She looked him up and down. "You saved my ass a bunch'a times when they was gonna fire me. Wait here."

It took her a few minutes to get what he wanted, and she came back out with a file. She handed it to him and said, "You didn't get this from me."

"Of course not. Thanks, I owe you one."

She mumbled something to herself as she walked away, and Stanton tucked the file under his arm as he headed out of the station.

The beach was crowded but not loud, filled mostly with young men and women sunbathing or surfing. Stanton sat in the sand and took off his shoes, letting the warmth penetrate the skin of his feet. He opened Ransom's file and began to read.

All the documents were copies, and some of them had smeared at the edges. The folder held over fifty pages. His employment history included many transfers during his career, and his disciplinary history had a few things on it.

Apparently, he had been brought up twice on brutality charges, and both investigations had been dropped because the victims stopped being cooperative. He quickly flipped through an Excel spreadsheet of Ransom's case history. Then Stanton found something he hadn't expected: a psychological history.

In 1983, after his divorce, Ransom had suffered a nervous breakdown and attempted suicide. He'd washed down a bottle of painkillers with whiskey. He'd slipped into a coma for three days and was suspended from the force for nearly a year before being cleared to return to work. Several years later, he met his current wife and had two boys. He had a son from his first marriage, but the file said nothing about him.

Stanton flipped through the rest of the file then returned to the beginning and went through everything again. After any attempted suicide, the officer involved had to complete a full psychological work-up, but that wasn't among the pages. He guessed that Ransom had taken care of that a long time ago. IAD had power unlike any other divisions.

When he was finished reading everything in the file, Stanton headed back to the station and worked a few of his other cases, following up leads and making calls to the toxicology labs to ask them to hurry things along. For the rape case at the bar, he got two undercovers from Vice to go down with one of the witnesses this weekend. He fully expected a positive ID, and he planned to bring the suspects down to the station and interview them himself.

When the day was over, he saw that the sun was still bright and wondered if he could fit in an hour of surfing but decided against it. He headed straight to Sandra's house and found her front door open.

"Hello?" he shouted from the doorway.

"Hey, I'm in here."

Stanton found her in the kitchen, making something over the stove.

"What are you cooking?"

"Chicken gumbo. You want some?"

"Sure."

He got a soda out of the fridge and sat down at the dining room table. Her house was on a hill that offered a view of the valley below, and he saw a few of her neighbors out on back porches, barbequing. He thought of his own barbeques with the boys and Melissa: Matt helping flip the burgers and Melissa getting onions and tomatoes ready. They always said a prayer before eating; Matt would emulate the way his father crossed his arms, and when it was done, he said "Amen" the loudest.

"Here ya go." She placed the food down in front of him and got some rolls out of the oven before sitting across from him.

"This is delicious. I didn't know you could cook."

"One of the only things I actually learned at home. I liked spending time with the help more than my parents, so I was always in the kitchen."

Stanton wiped his mouth with a napkin and took a long drink of water. "So what's going on, Sandra? Why are you wearing a wire?"

She placed her fork down, not looking at him. "I have some things I haven't discussed with you."

"Like what?"

"I... when I was with Vice, I did undercover work, and I reached that point, you know? That point where you have to make a choice how far you're willing to go to keep up the bullshit. I was offered some coke by some of the other working girls, and I thought it would be really weird if I didn't have some. We were trying to bust this really vicious pimp named Hidalgo. He was picking up fourteen- and fifteen-year-old girls and forcing them into gang bangs. That's what they do with new girls... to get them over their repulsion of sex at that age.

"After they raped them for weeks, they would send them out into the streets and in cities they didn't have any contacts in. All they had at that point was him. A lot of the girls ended up dead before they could get their driver's licenses. I really wanted to bust his ass, and I didn't want to raise any suspicions. I wanted the girls to trust me. So I did the coke."

"And you got hooked?"

She nodded.

"How often do you do it?"

"Not much. Really, not that much. Maybe once or twice every other day. But it's enough to never be a cop again. Being a cop's the only thing I was ever good at, Jon. I can't lose that."

"How'd Ransom find out you were using?"

"I don't know. You need to be careful with him. He's crazy. Something's wrong with him."

Stanton thought a moment before speaking. "Okay, here's what we do: You keep up the façade and gather info. Do whatever he asks. I don't have anything to hide, so he won't find anything. But you gotta get clean. I think you need to check in somewhere. There's a facility not far from—"

"Rehab? I'm not going to fucking rehab. I can handle it. I'll just stop. I promise." She reached out and touched his hand. "I promise, I'll stop."

When they had finished eating, Sandra cleaned up the dishes while Stanton sat on the sofa and watched television. She came in and stood against the wall, watching him as he smiled at the sitcom. He was like a boy in a way, a boy who refused to grow up because he knew what waited for him if he ever became an adult. It was one of the things she liked most about him.

She watched television with him for another twenty minutes before he kissed her goodnight and left. She saw him out and waited until he had pulled away before shutting the door. She went to the kitchen and stood over the sink. She took a bottle of whiskey from the cupboard and poured herself a shot.

Ransom stepped out of the bedroom and sat at the dining room table where Stanton had been sitting. He ran his hands along the edge, letting his fingers land on a handprint on the tabletop. "That was good. He trusts you."

She poured another shot and threw it back. "Yeah."

He walked over to her, took the bottle from her hand, and poured her another shot. He rested his chin on her shoulder, and she could tell he'd smelled her hair. He held the glass up to her lips, and she reluctantly drank.

"Do you believe that about me?" he asked softly. "That there's something wrong with me?"

"Yes." She pushed him away and turned to face him. "And I don't want to do this anymore."

"It's not just drugs, and we both know it, don't we?"

He stared into her eyes so long that she grew uncomfortable and looked away. "What do you want from me?"

"From you, nothing. But I want Jon Stanton sitting behind bars, where he belongs."

"He doesn't belong there."

"How the fuck would you know!"

He composed himself, bringing his fingers up to his eyes and squeezing lightly. "Sorry. Just do what you're told, and it'll be over soon."

She didn't turn around as he walked away, but when she heard the door close, she took another shot and began to cry.

28

Stanton met Taylor Rowe outside the Emerald Plaza building fifteen minutes early. The sun was already baking the city, and he felt beads of sweat across his forehead. He wished he hadn't worn a suit, but knew Coop would probably mention that during the deposition if he hadn't.

Rowe was dropped off in a Lincoln Town Car and stepped out, already on her phone. Dressed in a red business suit and heels, she looked as though she could've been on a runway somewhere.

"Jon, how are you?"

"Good."

She finished her call and tucked her phone into her bag. "We're just doing Daniel Childs's deposition today. I don't expect he has too much good information, so we'll probably only be here a few hours. Chin Ho was scheduled next, and Detective Porter after that, but there's been a change in plans. Your deposition is going to be on Friday. Coop requested it in exchange for a couple of stipulations on his part. We can get into that later, but it's a good trade. I need you to come by the office tonight so we can spend some time prepping."

"Sure."

"Okay, well, remember that everything here is on the record. Don't say anything unless I ask you to. Come on, they're waiting for us."

The Plaza was a beehive of buildings rather than a single tower. Stanton and Rowe took the elevator to the twenty-ninth floor and stepped off into a plush hallway. A small fountain was set up in the lobby next to the Offices of Gary C. Coop. The young, attractive secretary showed them back to the conference room, which was like a small auditorium. Stanton did a quick survey of the conference table, which was easily thirty-feet long, and counted twenty chairs. Flat screens had been hung wherever they would fit, and the exterior wall was tinted glass overlooking the city. Coop sat at the head of the table.

"Detective," Coop said as he stood, "have a seat."

Several other people were sitting at the table, but Stanton could identify only the court reporter acting as stenographer. He sat next to Rowe and watched as Coop sat back down, a slight grin on his lips.

"We're just waiting for Detective Childs," Coop said. "Would you like something to eat or drink in the meantime? We have bagels, juice, we can get an omelet from downstairs..."

"I'm fine, thank you."

They were silent another few minutes and Stanton peeked over at Rowe, who was on a tablet, reviewing the disciplinary section of Childs's HR history.

It was nearly twenty after when Childs came in. He was wearing a tight T-shirt that exposed his arms and slacks with a press crease; he didn't look any different than he would on any other given day, except that he was wearing his sidearm in a more prominent position on his waist.

"Detective Childs," Coop said, "nice of you to come."

"Fuck you, asshole." Childs sat down right next to Coop. "Let's get this bullshit over with."

Stanton saw a slight grimace on Coop's face. He didn't care for anyone else to be in control of the situation. Stanton also guessed Coop was upset that he hadn't had the stenographer dictating during that little barb from Childs.

However, other than the grimace, Coop handled the situation coolly and didn't react. He crossed his legs and picked up the legal pad he had written his questions on.

"Are we ready?" Coop asked the stenographer.

"We are."

"Okay. Please state your full name and address for the record, Detective."

"Sergeant Daniel William Childs, 1276 Westpoint, San Diego, California, 92103."

"And where do you work, and for how long?"

"San Diego Police Department, and I've been with them for sixteen years."

"What unit are you assigned to now?"

"I'm sergeant at the Northern Precinct. I'm supervisor over special squads and operations."

"Did you supervise or partake in the investigation which was dubbed 'The Sandman Murders'?"

"Yes."

"Could you please describe what the Sandman Murders were, Sergeant?"

"They were a series of three kidnappings involving young girls between the ages of ten and twelve. They weren't technically murders since no remains were ever found, but when a child is missing for over thirty days, they are presumed dead."

"And why were they called the Sandman Murders? Where did the term *Sandman* come from?"

"The girls were kidnapped from their homes between the hours of ten p.m. and two a.m. The term was applied by the newspapers when they covered the story, and it just stuck."

"And what were the names of the girls?"

"I don't know off the top of my head."

"You don't know? Were you not the supervisor in charge of this case?"

"I was, but that doesn't mean I was involved in it. The lead detective is the one who handles all the details."

"So what was your role?"

"As I said earlier, supervisory. If anything went wrong or if the investigation wasn't going in the right direction, I would step in and help."

"So who was the lead detective?"

"Detective Jon Stanton."

"Now, you were familiar with Detective Stanton long before the Sandman case, were you not?"

"I was."

"In fact, you were once slated to be partners with him, correct?"

"Yes."

"And why were you two never made partners?"

Stanton watched as he hesitated.

"Sergeant, please answer the question. Why were you two never made partners?"

"Because Stanton took a leave of absence from the force."

"Why did he do that?"

"He was having some personal troubles and needed time off."

"Personal trouble, Sergeant? Isn't it true Detective Stanton was institutionalized at the Shadow Oaks Treatment Center for psychiatric problems?"

Childs looked at Stanton. "Yes."

"And those psychiatric problems, where do you believe they stem from?"

"I would object," Rowe interjected. "Childs is not a psychologist, Gary. Move on."

"I'll rephrase that," Coop said. "Sergeant, did you ever know Jon Stanton to have psychiatric problems when you first met him?"

"No."

"Did something occur to change that?"

"You could say that."

"And what was it that occurred?"

"His former partner, Eli Sherman, was arrested for a series of murders. Jon was the one who caught him, and Eli nearly killed him, shot him in the chest. Jon was in intensive care almost two weeks. He retired from the force after that."

"Now, when you refer to Eli Sherman, you mean Detective Eli Sherman who was convicted and sentenced to life in prison for the murder and rape of two young women, correct?"

"Yes."

"And isn't it true, Sergeant, that the San Diego Police Department believes the actual number of slayings by Detective Sherman to be in the range of ten to twenty?"

"I guess."

"You guess, or it's true?"

"It's true we think there's more murders. We don't know how many."

"And Detective Sherman was partnered with Detective Stanton for how long?"

"They were together almost two years."

"And is it fair to say that in two years, partners have the opportunity to grow close to one another?"

"Sure."

"Because you're out on the street, risking your lives together—brothers in arms and all that?"

"Something like that."

"So is it fair to say that Detective Sherman and Detective Stanton were probably fairly close after two years of being partnered together?"

"I couldn't say. Every partnership is different."

"Okay, but it's a possibility that they were close?"

"Anything's possible."

"And after two years of riding together every day, it's probable they were at the least… friends or familiars?"

"Sure."

"And in that two years, did Detective Stanton ever come to you with concerns about Detective Sherman?"

"What kind of concerns?"

"Anything relating to his job or personal life? Anything indicating he may not be what he seemed?"

"No, he never came to me with anything like that."

"Did he ever go to any of your superiors with anything like that?"

"Not that I'm aware of."

"So it's fair to say he had no idea Eli Sherman was killing

young women?"

"Of course he didn't know."

"Now, in your opinion, Sergeant, someone like Detective Stanton, someone who was close to Detective Sherman, who probably shared most of his meals with him, who probably spent holidays with him, who spent long hours together with a serial killer every day and saw absolutely nothing wrong with him—in your opinion, wouldn't you say that's someone who doesn't have the best judgment?"

"None of us saw it coming with Sherman. He was smooth. He could fool his own mama. Blaming it on Jon is unfair and, frankly, indecent. Ask the wives of any serial killer, and they'll tell you they had no idea their husband was doing what he was doing."

"So you have a police officer, sanctioned to carry a gun and put people in jail, out murdering women, and all you can say is 'none of us saw it coming'? Wouldn't you agree that's bad judgment on all your parts?"

"No, I wouldn't."

As Childs grew visibly upset, Coop wrote furiously, probably follow-up questions. He no doubt knew he'd struck a nerve and was hoping to get Childs upset enough to hang himself.

"Childs has a temper," Stanton whispered to Rowe.

"I'm objecting to this, Gary," Rowe said. "There's no point. It's all speculation, and a jury won't hear any of it anyway."

"Objection noted. Unless you want to ring up the judge this early, I'm going to continue with it."

"No, that's fine." She leaned toward Stanton. "He can ask what he wants. I'll object to break his rhythm, but judges get really upset when they have to mediate a simple deposition. It's not good to call him on this."

"Now, Sergeant," Coop continued, "you have a serial killer wearing the uniform and investigating crimes, interacting with witnesses, going to court and testifying under oath, and eventually, he's caught—"

"By Detective Stanton."

"Yes, by Detective Stanton. Eventually, he's caught and convicted, and roughly two and a half years later, Police Chief Michael Harlow is also arrested, correct?"

"Yes."

"And, in fact, he was arrested in the largest police corruption scandal in this county's—and probably this state's—history, correct?"

"Yes."

"Chief Harlow was confiscating narcotics and having trusted members of the force re-sell them on the streets?"

"Yes."

"And these trusted members, some of them sergeants like yourself, would sell these drugs back to the dealers they confiscated them from?"

"Yes."

"And he and these trusted members of the police force would then split the profits?"

"Yes."

"Did you ever get a piece of these profits?"

"No. Not once. And if I'd known about it, I'd have arrested Harlow myself."

"Did Detective Stanton ever get a piece of these profits?"

"No."

"So you have Detective Sherman out murdering women, and you have no idea, but you're telling me that you know for certain that Detective Stanton didn't skim a little profit from Harlow's drug trade? You know that for an absolute fact?"

Childs hesitated. "Not for an absolute fact, no. But I know Jon, and I know—"

"Just answering the question will suffice, Sergeant. Thank you. Now how many officers would you say were getting a piece of the money from the drug trade?"

"No idea."

"Not even a guess?"

"Nineteen officers were arrested, and seventeen convicted."

"How many would you say were not arrested?"

"I don't know."
"Would you say there were more than five?"
"I don't know."
"More than fifteen?"
"I don't know."
"More than twenty?"
"I don't fucking know! Damn, move on."
"Sergeant, please calm down and remain seated."
"I am seated. What the fuck are you talking about?"
"Sergeant, would you like a minute to calm down? Maybe take a break?"
"No, I'm fine."
"Okay," Coop said, a slight smirk on his face as he wrote something down.

Rowe leaned over to Stanton. "He told him to remain seated because the jury is only going to read the transcript. There's no video to see that he never got out of his seat. It makes him look crazy."

"Now, Sergeant," Coop continued, "I'd like to turn to the Sandman case. Now you said Detective Stanton was the lead detective. How did he identify my client's son, Darrell Putnam, as the perpetrator of those crimes?"

"The three victims lived near each other. We did a sex offender search and hit on fourteen names. Putnam's previous crimes fit."

"Fit how?"
"He was a child sex offender with two priors."
"How long ago were those crimes committed?"
"The first one was fifteen years ago, and the second one was eight years ago."
"And he did prison time on each of those and was released?"
"Yes."
"Did he kill either of those vics in his previous offenses?"
"No."
"Did he kidnap them in the middle of the night?"
"No."

Coop made a few more notes then put down his pen. "I think that's all I have for you now, Sergeant. I may re-call you to another deposition further down the line should something develop." Coop signaled to the stenographer to cut the recording. She stopped taking dictation and turned off the audio. "And, brother, you need to calm down. You lie with whores, you gonna wake up with whores. Ain't no reason to get upset with me."

Childs stood up. "We got the same skin color, but you ain't my brother. And you're the only whore I see here."

He stormed out without looking back, and Stanton looked at Rowe. She closed out her tablet and stood up. "See you Friday."

Stanton followed her out as Coop sent him a glare then smiled.

29

Stanton knocked on Melissa's front door, and she answered in sweats.

"Hey, handsome," she said, kissing him on the cheek. "What's going on?"

"Nothing. I just wanted to see you."

"I was just working out. Come in."

The house looked immaculate, and a cardio kickboxing DVD was playing on the television in the front room. She turned it off, went to the kitchen, and returned with two bottles of water. They sat on the couch awhile, not saying anything. Stanton dropped by like this every so often, and they had grown accustomed to it.

"How was your morning?" Melissa asked.

"Not that great. I was in a deposition."

"Over the Sandman thing?"

"Yeah."

"I heard the mother is asking for millions of dollars. Not much of a mother if your son grows up and kidnaps little kids. She doesn't deserve a dime."

"Maybe, but you never know with a jury."

"You actually think you might lose?"

"I don't know. I'm not sure what I think right now." He set his bottle on the coffee table and leaned forward, his elbows against his knees, his hands rubbing together as if they were cold, despite the warmth. "I'm not sure this is worth it anymore, Mel. It seems like most days I'm just bashing my head against a wall, and the harder I bash, the more I get punished for it. I don't think I want this anymore."

"We've had this conversation before, Jon."

"I know."

"And you've gone back on your word each time."

"I know that, too."

"I can't get my hopes up again. Neither can the kids. I know what you want. You want me to tell you to move back in and to start making plans. That you're going to be a professor, and we're going to live this perfect life. That's not going to happen. You've broken my heart too many times. I won't let it happen again."

"What can I do to make you believe me?"

"Quit right now. Call your boss and give your resignation. Don't tell him why—just do it. And don't go back. We'll have someone else go back and get your things."

"Mel, I—"

"I know, you can't. That's the problem, Jon. That's why I don't believe you."

"It's this last case. The wrong guy's been blamed—I know it. I can feel it. The monster's still out there, and we're not even looking for him. If I quit, he'll disappear and take who knows how many kids with him."

"That's what you don't understand, Jon. It's what you've never understood: there's always more monsters. The world has always been a mess and always will be a mess. The point is to straighten out your own life."

"You might be right, but that's not going to comfort me when we're watching television and an Amber alert flashes across the bottom of the screen. I'll always wonder if it was him. For the rest of my life, I would wonder. I don't want that to be who I am. I'm going to either catch him or kill him, but I can't just let him go."

She watched him a moment, then leaned over and kissed his cheek. "You go do what you need to do. I just can't promise that I can wait."

She took his hand and rose, and he stood with her, allowing her to lead him to the door. They stood on the threshold, looking out. Young kids were playing across the street. Stanton wanted so badly to say, *See. Look at them. Look at what he's taking out of the world. How can you ask me to just allow it?* Instead, he kissed Melissa once more, then walked to his car.

At 2:10 p.m., Stanton pulled to a stop near Woodrow Wilson Elementary. He parked up the street, but close enough to see the entire perimeter, except for a dozen or so feet blocked by one of the buildings. After deciding that blind spot was too large, he got out and walked to the gap in the fence that led to the front entrance of the school.

The kids began to pile out, and Stanton only casually glanced at them, pretending he was a waiting parent. He was more interested in the other adults around the school. On the south side, a group of five young men, who were perhaps no older than seventeen, loitered about. His profile of the abductor did not fit a group attack, which would have been more violent and obvious as each member attempted to impress the others with his lack of morality and compassion. The Sandman kidnappings were subtle and quiet; they were the work of a single person who was probably ashamed of what he was doing but had an eye toward making a long career of doing it.

Stanton took a few steps south and leaned against the fence, careful not to look too long at any one person. Then he saw a couple of young boys run into the crowd of seventeen-year-olds. One of the older boys hugged one of the younger, and the younger one handed him a paper. They were likely brothers.

There was no one else around the perimeter of the school.

This was a bust.

Just as Stanton was about to turn away, he saw movement out of the corner of his eye. A man had run over from across the street and was sitting on a bicycle rack on the west side of the school. He was older than the group of boys, perhaps twenty-three or twenty-four, and was staring at the girls as they walked by.

Stanton's heart raced. He pulled out his phone and buried his face in it as he hiked along the sidewalk toward the west side of the school. He didn't glance up, except to ensure he had a clear path. He looked once at the street when he heard screeching tires—a mother on her cell had come to an abrupt stop, nearly running over some kids at a crosswalk. The man had noticed, too, and he looked at Stanton.

Stanton glanced away as quickly as possible, but he was too late. He stuck out too much. The man hopped off the bicycle rack and began walking toward the intersection.

Stanton picked up his pace and put away his phone, giving up on the charade. The man didn't turn around until he got to the intersection about seventy feet ahead of Stanton. He turned around, looked at Stanton, then sprinted across the street.

Stanton shouted, "Stop, police!" and ran.

The man was at a full sprint. Stanton came to a red light. Cars were coming from both sides. He dashed across, and one driver laid on the horn while slamming on the brakes and twisting to the side, hitting a bus in the far left lane.

Stanton continued running as the other cars came to a standstill. The driver of the car he'd caused to hit the bus was out and chasing him, but he had no time to stop. The man in front of him had just turned a corner, and Stanton couldn't see him.

He rushed past a group of children walking home and nearly toppled a homeless man pushing a shopping cart. When he rounded the corner, Stanton saw the man hop a chain-link fence and run into a house. Stanton sprinted for him and vaulted over the fence. He raced up the old porch steps and tried to open the front door. It was locked.

He stepped back, lifted his leg, and bashed his heel against the door, just underneath the doorknob. The door didn't budge. He kicked it again and again, but nothing happened. There was a window just to the side of the porch. He grabbed a patio chair and sent it crashing through the window.

He used another chair to scrape away as much of the glass remaining on the window frame as he could, then climbed through. The house was empty except for trash on the floors: old fast-food containers, beer bottles, condom wrappers... Stanton suspected it was a vacant house where local teens went to get drunk. He didn't see the hypodermic needles or vomit and fecal stains of a full-blown drug house.

He ran through the living room then stopped in the hall and listened. The house was quiet, and dust swirled in the sunbeams coming through the cracks in the boarded-up windows. He held his breath and closed his eyes...

A soft brushing sound came from upstairs. He pulled out his firearm and held it low as he climbed the stairs to the second floor. The carpet had been torn up, exposing multi-colored foam padding underneath. The walls were covered with graffiti, and the unmistakable stench of marijuana hung in the air. Stanton walked down the hallway, pausing after each step to listen. He consciously tried to slow his pounding heart, as if someone might hear it.

There was a crash in the room next to him, and Stanton raised his weapon. A piece of ripped-up floorboard that had been leaning against the wall of the bathroom had fallen over. Stanton put his back to the wall in the hallway and reached into the bathroom to flip on the light.

The tub was filled with rancid water, urine, cigarette butts, old beer, and who knew what else. It stank like sulfur and animal entrails, and Stanton dry-heaved. He turned away, and as he did so, a chair came up and smashed into his face.

He flew back into the tub, splashing water onto the floor. The chair came down again, and he held up his forearm. The impact felt like a jackhammer. The man lifted and smashed again, just missing Stanton's head. Stanton ducked into the water, and the chair slammed against the edges of the tub. He came up with his firearm and pressed it into the man's groin.

"Don't," Stanton said, out of breath, shaking putrid water

out of his eyes. "Unless you don't care if you have any kids."

"You won't fuckin' do it."

"Why not? Haven't you heard? I kill criminals for fun."

The man looked at him a few moments then dropped the chair to the floor.

30

Stanton knew the young man was sitting in the interrogation room. Stanton had wanted to go in to question him, but his dunk in the filthy tub convinced him to station a uniform outside the interrogation room while he showered in the locker room.

He dumped the clothes he had been wearing in the trash. His cell phone, luckily, still worked but he'd probably have to see a doctor considering he still had open wounds. But he decided it could wait and went to the cafeteria. He bought a drink and sat alone at one of the tables. He had vomited several times before and after uniforms had come to the house to pick up the suspect. He sipped a Fresca to settle his queasy stomach. When the can was empty, he headed to the interrogation room.

The man, Cameron Spangler, had his head down on the table, buried in his folded arms. He looked up as Stanton walked in. "I didn't do nothin'."

"You assaulted a police officer with a deadly weapon."

"It was a chair."

"Could'a fooled me. It felt like a bat." Stanton had brought in a file under his arm, and he placed it on the table as he sat down. He opened it and brought out the photos of the young girls. He placed them in front of Cameron and let it sit awhile.

Cameron glanced at two of them, stared at Sarah's picture, then buried his head again. "I'm not saying anything."

"You don't have to. There are officers at your mom's house, executing a search warrant right now. I'm sure we'll find everything we need there."

He looked up. "What the fuck are you doing at my mom's house?"

"We'll get to your house, too. Don't worry. But I know people like you, Cameron. I know them really well, and I know you keep your best trinkets at your mom's. And when they find them, you're going to prison for a long time. Maybe even to a date with a needle."

He made a dismissive sound and put his head down again.

Stanton took a deep breath and stood up. "Follow me."

"No."

"I can have the officer out there tie you like a pig and drag you, or you can follow me. Your choice."

Cameron slowly stood up.

Stanton took him past the drunk tank to the holding cells farthest away from everybody else. This was where they kept the prisoners awaiting arraignments and transfer to the county facilities. In the farthest two cells, they kept the inmates considered too dangerous to be with the others: the ones who no longer had any fear of incarceration and might mutilate or rape other inmates.

Stanton stopped in front of the cell and brought Cameron over. The inmate came to the bars and stuck his hands through. He was bald and covered in tattoos, but his chubby face and glasses gave him a milder appearance.

"You bring me a treat, Jon?"

"This is Cameron. He might be joining you soon." He turned to Cameron. "This is Rich. I've known him for almost a decade. He can be your cellie for the next seventy-two hours if I want him to be. Rich here had to be confined by himself because last time he was here, he raped his cellie and scooped his eye out with a spoon." Stanton turned to Rich. "This is off the record. I give my word."

"Okay."

"What would you do if I put Cameron in that cell with you?"

He smiled. Several of his teeth were missing, and the remaining stumps were darkly stained and yellowed. "Oh, we'd have a good time, me and him. I need to bust a nut, anyway. You suck cock, fish? You'd learn with me. But if you bite, I'm gonna knock yer fucking teeth out, and then you ain't bite no more."

Stanton looked at Cameron and saw the terror. His hands were trembling, and he stared at the floor, unable to lift his eyes. Stanton grabbed him and led him away as Rich shouted about what they would do together. He pounded the bars like an animal, then began to hiss and spit. Stanton got Cameron back into the interrogation room and sat down across from him.

"That was set up," Cameron said. "That ain't real."

"Rich is real. He's schizophrenic. That's why he keeps getting released. When he took out the guy's eye last time, we couldn't find it in the cell. We think he might've eaten it."

Cameron swallowed hard, as if his throat were dry, and leaned forward, his elbows against the table. "What do you want to know?"

31

Stanton stepped out under the guise of getting them some sodas and made sure the video recorder was on in the interrogation room.

Slim Jim walked by, sucking on an unlit cigar. "Who you got in there?"

"Just some follow up."

"Follow up to what?"

"Routine case, nothing interesting."

"Whew, I know it's interesting when Jon Stanton is being evasive. I'm in. I wanna be bad cop."

"It's not like that. He's already agreed to talk. I was just making sure the camera's working."

"Well, can I second, at least?"

"I don't think so, Jim."

"All right. I got better stuff to do anyways."

Stanton went back in the room with a pad and pen. He pushed some photos toward Cameron and leaned back in his chair, purposely putting his hands on the table in an open position. Crossed arms tended to signify disbelief in what the speaker was saying.

"That girl—her name is Sarah—I want to know about her. When did you meet her?"

"That's that chick that got kidnapped, huh? I only met her once, at one of Tracey's parties."

"Tracey Adams?"

"Yeah. Hey, where are those drinks?"

"I didn't have enough change. I told someone to bring them.

What were Tracey's parties like?"

"They were crazy." He hesitated. "I don't know if... I think I want to ask to not be arrested on this stuff."

"You're asking for immunity, and I'll consider it. If you help me, I'll definitely help you."

"There was a lot crazy stuff there, man. Like chicks way young, like these here, and there were lines'a coke on the table and people in masks just fucking right in front of you. Crazy shit."

"Where were these parties held?"

"Tracey's house. Her mom was the one that would have them."

Slim Jim opened the door and walked in with two sodas. He placed them down, smiled at Cameron with a slight nod, then walked out.

"She knew there were young girls there?" Stanton asked.

"Oh yeah, man. She was the one that would pay me to pick 'em up. But that's all I did. Tracey was like friends with 'em, and her mom, Angie, would tell me to go pick them up."

"Is that what you were doing at the school today?"

"Yeah."

"So why'd you run if you were just picking somebody up?"

He shrugged. "I don't know. I just ran. I was scared. I thought I could get in trouble even though all I did was pick them up."

"So you'd pick them up from school, take them to the Adams' house, and then what would happen?"

"They'd get drunk or high, and we'd chill for a bit. Then Tracey's mom would come down and start teachin' 'em about sex. I would watch, but I never did nothin'."

"There were drunk girls there willing to have sex, and you expect me to believe you never did anything with them?"

"I don't... I'm not into that."

"Into what?"

"Girls."

"Okay, well, let's assume I believe you for now. How many parties were there?"

"Um, like five so far. We're supposed to have one tonight. That's why I was there to pick up this chick."

"Which chick?"

"Her name was Kim. I don't know her last name."

"If I go over to the Adams' house tonight, am I going to find them in the middle of a party?"

"Yeah."

"What time would be best for me to see what's happening?"

"Like probably around ten."

"Okay, wait here."

Stanton stepped out of the interrogation room to find Slim Jim and Childs standing there, listening through the two-way mirror set up as a window in the room. Childs looked at him and shook his head.

"I told you no more Sandman case."

"You heard what he said. How could I not follow up?"

"Because I fucking told you not to. I am your *boss*. Do you get that?"

"Yeah, but that was the wrong call, Danny. I had to do it."

He exhaled loudly through his nose and looked at Cameron through the mirror. "We're gonna raid that fucking house tonight, and tomorrow morning, I want you in my office first thing. Got it?"

"Yeah."

"Slim Jim, go get me a warrant. I want three uniforms and three detectives besides Jon."

"Got it, boss."

"Jon, I want you to go in there and tell him to go to that party and act like nothing's wrong. He's also gonna have to wear a wire."

"I wouldn't recommend that."

"Why the hell not?"

"He's nervous and weak. He can't handle the pressure of a wire."

"I disagree. Get him sounded up."

"Danny, he can't do it. Let's just have him call and say he

couldn't find the girl, but he found another one that he's bringing later."

"Do as I fucking say, Detective. Or you can just go home."

32

Stanton sat in a van outside the Adams' house at ten o'clock, along with a tech, Slim Jim, and Cameron. He watched the moon through the van's back windows for a long time. Something about a full moon appealed to a man's sense of peace—as well as his sense of madness. He didn't know if there was anything else like that, with the exception of women.

"This fucking hurts," Cameron said.

The tech was taping the wire to his chest. "It's gonna hurt worse when you rip it off."

"It itches."

"Well, be glad I'm not taping it to your balls then."

Slim Jim snorted out a laugh and kicked over an empty soda can on the floor. "And I was just gonna sit home and watch reruns of *Battlestar Galactica* tonight."

"Slim Jim, you ready to go?"

He got on the horn. "Ready, Lieutenant."

"Send him in."

Stanton opened the back doors and helped Cameron hop out. He stepped outside with him and stood there for a while, looking up at the house. He imagined Bob at a sports bar with his friends, thinking about the beautiful wife waiting for him at home, figuring she was in bed, watching television.

"Listen to me, Cameron. You don't need to do anything out of the ordinary. Just go in and hang out. We'll be in soon, and we're going to act like we've never met. You'll be arrested, and I'm going to be the one to do it, okay?"

"Okay."

"You're doing the right thing here. You're going to have a future and a life because of it."

"I don't... I don't know if I should be doing this, you know? Maybe I shouldn't."

"Too late to go back now. It's going to be easy. Angie's who I want, not you."

"Okay." He took a deep breath. "How do I look?"

"Like a rock star."

He turned and walked the half block to the home as Stanton climbed back into the van.

Slim Jim looked at him and smiled. "Does he know he's just as liable for the rape of those kids as Angie?" he asked Stanton.

"No."

"There's no way Childs is gonna not pursue that. He's gonna slam that kid hard."

"Danny tends to take it easy on people who cooperate. If we can get a good word in with the DA, too, he'll probably be okay."

"*Okay*? Okay in the sense that he might get out of prison one day, I guess. Don't justify it to yourself, Jon. The guy's a piece of shit and deserves what's comin' to him."

"Shh," the tech said, attempting to pick up the signal from the wire.

Stanton heard music then conversation underneath, but the music was so loud, making out distinct words was impossible.

"He needs to go to a quiet room," Slim Jim said.

"He doesn't realize the music's too loud."

The conversation lasted perhaps another five minutes, most of it inaudible because of the music. Then there was some commotion, and the music began to die down. Eventually, it was little more than thumping bass. Stanton could hear liquid being mixed followed by a faucet running for a bit. A fridge opened.

"How come you couldn't pick up Kim?" a female's voice asked.

"She wasn't there. I waited for like twenty minutes."

"I told her you were coming to pick her up. That's really weird. I hope she's okay."

"That's got to be her," Slim Jim said.

"We'll have to get her next time. She's a little princess."

"How'd you meet her?" Cameron asked.

Good boy, Stanton thought.

"She's one of Tracey's tutoring students. She's over here all the time. I told her parents we're having movie night over here, and she'd be back by midnight. Want some coke?"

"No, I'm not feeling very good."

"What's wrong?"

"I don't know, just sick. So do you have enough girls here?"

"Yeah, there's some cheerleaders here. I think they're already drunk in the hot tub. You wanna come watch us?"

"No, I'm okay."

"Slim Jim," Childs's voice crackled through the horn. "Time to move."

"Got it." He turned to Stanton. "Let's go."

They checked their Kevlar vests and jumped out of the van. They didn't expect any gunplay, but the regulations were clear, and Stanton didn't want anything to go wrong, not while he was under investigation by IAD.

As Stanton and Slim Jim ran up the sidewalk toward the house, officers sprinted up the other side of the lawn to the front door. Two other officers rounded the side of the house to cover the back door. The rest gathered on the front porch, and Childs was carrying the ram used to smash open locked doors. He held up his fingers, counting down.

Three. Two. One.

Childs bashed the ram through the door while shouting, "Police, search warrant!"

The door flew open. Down the hall, in the living room, several young girls screamed. The officers rushed in with weapons drawn and secured the room. Stanton saw Cameron in the kitchen with Angie, and he ran in and lifted his firearm. He threw Cameron against the fridge and pinned him there. He had just turned to tell Angie to get down on the floor when he saw her reach into a drawer and pull out a handgun.

Stanton let go of Cameron. They stood motionless, Stanton staring down at the barrel of the weapon pointed at his chest. Every fiber in his body told him to go for a kill shot if he had to fire—his training had emphasized that the only time to draw a weapon was when you intended to use it—but he couldn't bring himself to. He lowered the weapon a few inches, aiming at her pelvic bone. It would be extremely painful, but she would live.

"Drop your weapon," he ordered.

"No."

She was frantic; he could see it in her eyes. She looked like a cornered animal that knew it was about to die.

"There's nothing you can do, Angie. There's half a dozen cops in your house and more on the way. Drop the gun, and we can sit down and talk."

"I want my lawyer."

"You'll get your lawyer. I promise you. But you have to drop the gun first."

"No, no, go get my lawyer, and then I'll put the gun down."

"Doesn't work like that, Angie. I need you to drop the weapon right now."

She looked behind her as two officers made their way in through the back door and looked toward the kitchen. Her eyes were wide. She was in hysterics. Stanton could sense that she would fire; she didn't know what else to do.

He lowered his weapon and holstered it. "See, I've put my gun away. You're not in any danger. We just need you to drop the gun, and then we're gonna get your lawyer over here, and you can talk to us or not talk to us. Up to you."

She stepped toward the counter. "I want my husband, too."

"Him, too."

She hesitated. "Okay, okay. I'm gonna put the gun down on the counter, but you don't move."

"I won't move. I promise."

She only managed to take a couple of steps before the uniforms both raised their weapons and began shouting orders at her. Stanton saw the look in her eyes, and as she turned with the gun in her hand toward the officers, he yelled, "No!"

They fired four rounds in quick succession. Three hit her in the chest and one in the head just above her right eye. Stanton sprinted toward her and cradled her in his arms. He ripped off his vest and tore his shirt, placing it on her chest and pushing to keep the blood contained.

But the wound in her head spurted dark blood like a fountain, and it pooled on the linoleum of the kitchen.

"Call an ambulance!"

33

Stanton sat outside Assistant Chief Chin Ho's office and took two Advil without water. The cellophane wrapping crinkled as he smashed it in his palm then threw it in the waste bin near him. It was ten in the morning, and he hadn't slept the night before. He'd stayed awake, watching the moonlight dance on the ceiling.

"Detective," the receptionist said, "they're ready for you."

Stanton walked into the office, where three men were waiting. Ho was sitting at the desk, and Childs was seated on the couch, looking out the window. Ransom Talano stood behind Ho, his arms folded.

"Detective Stanton," Ho said, "sit down please."

He sat and crossed his legs, leaning back in the chair. The office was cooler than the rest of the building. It was decorated with medals and framed photos of past chiefs. In the corner was a small statue of Justice holding the scales.

Chin Ho took a newspaper off his desk and slid it across to Stanton. It was a copy of today's *Union-Trib*. The headline read "San Diego's Angel of Death," and a photo of Stanton was printed underneath the top caption.

"Have you read this?" Ho asked.

"No, but I can guess what it says."

"You can guess? And how can you guess?"

"The woman who was killed was a client of Gary Coop. He's got contacts everywhere. I'm sure this is a hack job, considering he's suing us right now. He's trying to taint the jury pool."

"It is a hack job. And a damn good one. He paints you as some kind of maniac and us as accomplices."

"She made her choice. She wouldn't drop the weapon."

"What about Darrell Putnam?" Ransom chimed in. "Did he make his choice, too?"

"Yes."

"You've had two deaths weeks apart, Jon," Ho said. "The two officers involved were suspended with pay. Same for you. Please hand over your badge and gun to the sergeant before you leave."

"I didn't shoot her, Chin."

"I know. But you were the commanding officer on scene. It was your responsibility."

Stanton rose. He placed his firearm and badge on the desk. "Keep them. I don't want them back."

Stanton stepped out of the precinct building, and a smile came over his face. He lifted his head toward the sun and felt its warmth envelope him. He felt as if his chains had been lifted. He felt weightless, like he could go anywhere and do anything, and he didn't want that to end.

He took out his phone and called Melissa.

"Hey," she said.

"I quit."

There was a long pause on the other end. He waited for what seemed like minutes before breaking the silence.

"Mel?"

"I'm here. What happened?"

"You haven't seen the paper?"

"No, I'm just getting the kids ready for school."

"Go online and check out the *Union-Trib*. They'll hear about it at school, so you should explain it to them now. I was involved in a shooting that ended in someone dying. Tell them I tried to save her."

"I will. When can you come over?"

"In a couple of hours."

"Okay. I'll see you then."

"Okay."

"Jon?"

"Yeah, I'm still here."

"I'm proud of you."

He couldn't speak for a moment. "Thanks. I'll see you in a bit."

As he got into his car, he thought about what his life was going to be now. His schedule as a professor had been flexible and had allowed him to leave early to take his boys to Padres baseball games or to catch afternoon movies. He'd never been stressed because he knew exactly what to expect the next day.

After retiring from the force following the incident with Sherman, Stanton had had trouble sleeping. Images of the dead filled his dreams and called out to him. One dream in particular was especially memorable: he was on a lounge chair on the beach while the setting sun filled the sky with a golden glow. The water foamed in large clouds, and the sand was smooth, untouched.

He was making love to a slender blonde woman in a red dress. She was barefoot as she lifted her dress and cradled him around the waist. Her skin was soft, and she kissed him so hard he couldn't breathe. She pulled away, and he saw that her face was just exposed skull, framed by flowing blonde hair.

At that point, he would wake, his shirt clinging to him with sweat, his heart pounding. Sometimes, he went back to sleep, but most nights, he couldn't. But when he returned to teaching, the dreams faded a little each day, until one night, he didn't dream at all. A few nights after that, he dreamed about his family and the ocean. Eventually, the dream with the blonde stopped altogether.

In the past year and a half, it had returned.

Stanton started the car, anxious to get away from the precinct. He was planning to go home, surf until sunset, then take his wife and kids to a big dinner anywhere they wanted to go. Then they would stay up late and watch movies. He would pop popcorn, and with any luck, Melissa would allow him to stay the night.

As the engine turned, he noticed something on his passenger seat. He looked over to see the open file, and ten-year-old Sarah's picture lying out.

34

Calvin Riley saw a puppy on the corner, and it excited him. When he was a kid, his grandparents' neighbors had many dogs and cats, and it was a quiet, safe neighborhood where they felt they could allow their pets to roam. He had started with insects, but they had no expressions. Cats and dogs had expressions, and he liked to watch them as he cut them apart in his grandfather's basement. He took photos once, and his mother had discovered them. He was never left alone to play outside there again.

The newspaper arrived eleven minutes late. Calvin knew he had access to any news he wanted online, but something about holding an actual paper in his hands made him feel adult—and important, somehow.

"You're late," he said to the man who had hopped out of the truck and was loading papers into a bin.

"What?"

"I said you're late."

"Piss off."

Calvin glanced around and saw that no one was near. He grabbed the man by the forearm then brought the man's other arm up around his back, putting his own hand on the man's neck. He slammed the man's head into the bin. Calvin had him pinned there, applying pressure to his arm the more he resisted.

"You need to learn to be nicer," he said. "You never know what people are capable of."

A couple stepped out of a shop nearby, and Calvin let the man go. He took a paper and threw a crumpled-up dollar in the man's face. He walked back to his Beetle and got into the driver's seat. He wanted to read the paper right away, but he decided he wanted to feel the anticipation more. He planned to read it when he got home.

He drove slowly on the freeway in the far right lane. He rolled down all his windows and let the warm air fill the car. He glanced at the passenger door, and the lock caught his eye. It was scratched from when he had unsuccessfully attempted to make it a one-way lock so no one could open it from inside the car. He had briefly considered taking it to a mechanic, but he knew that was something a mechanic would remember.

When he got home, he parked in the garage and ran inside the house. He heard his mother in the kitchen and snuck upstairs to his room. Quietly, he shut the door, kicked off his shoes, and lay in bed. He pulled out the newspaper, flipped to the Op/Ed section, and began to read the article:

San Diego's Angel of Death
By
Neil Brass
Staff Writer

When I was fourteen, I walked home through the Edgewater neighborhood in Miami, Florida. I had been at a dance, and my date had decided there were better fish in the sea. She'd gone home with one of the basketball players whose name I wish I could mention here (he's now a professional mover, so life does have a sense of justice).

I had rounded a corner near a small deli when a car came screeching to a halt across the street. Two men sprung out and opened the back doors. They pulled out a man who was covered in blood from head to toe. He was wearing a leather jacket, and I remembered thinking what an ugly color of brown the jacket was. They pulled the man down the street, past a lamppost, and I saw that his jacket was actually white but was so soaked with blood that it appeared brown.

The two men threw the third guy into an alley and gave him the worst beating I have ever seen (not counting a Lakers/Cavs game). They pummeled his head, his chest, his stomach, and even his arms and legs, when he tried to use them to block their vicious blows.

Finally, when they figured he'd had enough, one of the men grabbed a baseball bat out of the trunk and broke the man's legs at the knees. The two then got into the car and drove away. I was horrified.

I had never seen a fight that had drawn blood. And here was this man, lying in the alley, bleeding to death—and no one was around to see it but me.

I looked both ways down the street, and there were no cars. It was just me and this guy. I was maybe four blocks from home. I could go home, forget about him, and just have it be a little mystery in my life.

But conscience got the better of me. I ran across the street and checked the guy's pulse, mostly because I had seen people do it in movies. His heart was still beating, but he was unconscious, and blood was pouring out of the wounds on his face. I ran down the block to a bar that was open, and I had the bouncer run back with me. He called emergency services.

The next day, a detective from the organized crime section of the Miami-Dade County Sheriff's Office came to my house. I'll never forget him. His name was Detective Macks, and he was easily the biggest man I had ever seen. We sat on my porch and talked about what I had witnessed. Macks was calm and patient, and he told me that I was a hero for what I'd done. The man who was beaten had done nothing wrong.

"What are you gonna do when you catch the guys?" I asked.

"Nothing," Macks said. "My only job is to catch them."

Macks did catch his men. And true to his word, neither one of them was harmed. Macks testified against them in court, and when it was my turn, he sat in the courtroom the whole time then walked me out. When the trial ended and the scumbags were sentenced to ten years apiece, Macks took me out for an ice cream (a little weird for a fourteen-year-old, I know, but he was old school).

I remember Macks because he is what a cop should be. He busted two thugs in the Cuban Syndicate, and no one got hurt. He did his job and went home for the night. I wish we could say the same for our boys in blue right here in sunny San Diego.

The nightmare of the Michael Harlow administration has left a scar on our police force that seems to tear open every few months, revealing a fresh allegation of corruption or brutality. Harlow was, to put it plainly, the most corrupt son of a bitch to ever wear the uniform in this county. But he wasn't alone.

Most of his henchmen have been rooted out and brought to justice, but a few linger. Most notable among them: Assistant Chief Chin Ho and Detective Jonathan Stanton. For the most part, the assistant chief has kept a low profile. He moved up from the field quickly and has adjusted to life behind a desk with the quiet resolve we expect of our police force. But Jonathan Stanton—well, that's another story.

You may remember Detective Stanton from several years back. When he joined our police force, the speed and depth of his manner of solving cases made more than a few people stand up and take notice (there was even talk, believe it or not, of his possibly being psychic). But that Detective Stanton has gone the way of VCRs and Beta. The new Detective Stanton is a killing machine.

The Sandman Murders held this city by the throat for months, and we thought we could put another win in Stanton's column with the identification of Darrell Putnam, an unemployed iron worker who lived with his mother, as the culprit. And Detective Stanton chased him down like a bloodhound, resulting in his death.

The only problem is: Darrel Putnam didn't do it.

This paper has obtained internal memoranda from the SDPD relating to the ongoing investigation of the Sandman cases. To put it bluntly, folks, Stanton killed the wrong guy. The Sandman cases are still unsolved.

Not a month later, the death of Angie Adams has rocked the sleepy city out of its stupor. A housewife and mother of three, Angie was shot numerous times by a group of police officers led by Detective Stanton while she was hosting a party for her children.

This has to stop. We cannot have a maniac with the right to carry a gun and a badge murder two innocent people and then get away with it. Eventually, he will get what's coming to him. But in the meantime, are we supposed to suffer through botched investigations and murders?

This reporter says HELL NO!

Write the police chief, the commissioner, the mayor, the governor, your legislators, your congressmen—hell, write your old teachers and priests. Write anybody who will listen and tell them that we will no longer tolerate cops murdering innocent civilians in our city.

Calvin put down the paper and placed his hands behind his head as he looked up at the ceiling. The editorial, no doubt, was filled with half-truths and misdirection, and Calvin wouldn't have cared about it, except for a single line: "The Sandman cases are still unsolved."

Calvin ran that line through his head over and over until it made him sick. Darrell Putnam had been the guy. *What have they found to make them think otherwise?*

He jumped out of bed and went to what used to be a den but was now just a room where his mother kept the clutter. Calvin sat in the rusted office chair in front of the computer the family shared. He searched for Jonathan Stanton and found several articles relating to his closed cases.

He had closed cases everyone else had considered impossible. Stanton had even closed a few cold-case homicides, one almost twenty-five years old. A few articles mentioned his personal life. One said he was an avid surfer.

There was an old black-and-white photo of him at a crime

scene in a wooded area. Calvin stared at the photo a long time, burning every curve and surface of Stanton's face into his mind.

After reading for nearly an hour, Calvin turned off the computer and leaned back in the chair, staring up at a Led Zeppelin poster, advertising a concert no one in his family had gone to.

The Sandman cases are still unsolved.

Calvin took a deep breath and stood up to get to his car. He was going to have to meet this Jonathan Stanton.

35

Dusk had already fallen when Stanton arrived at the seafood restaurant on the beach. Several luxury cars were parked near the entrance, and a young kid was acting as the valet though he didn't have an ID or a uniform.

Stanton went inside and found it packed. The restaurant had a window for every table, and the sunshine and fresh sea air came through the screens of the open windows. The wait staff was young but friendly enough. Stanton saw Sandra sitting by herself near the back, and he headed toward her.

The walls were covered with black-and-white photos of fishing expeditions, nets, fishing rods, snow shoes, and a few plastic sharks and swordfish. Sandra was taking it all in passively, without showing any real interest.

Stanton sat across from her without a word, and she pushed the Diet Coke she had ordered for him across the table.

He took a sip then cleared his throat. "We can't see each other anymore," he said.

She stared at him a moment before replying, "Why not?"

"I'm getting back together with my wife. I quit the force today, and I just want to put this side of my life away. I'm enormously fond of you, Sandy. You know that. But I need to be with my wife and kids."

She dipped her straw in her drink, and it came back out glistening and wet. "To be honest, I kinda thought this was over. You didn't seem as interested anymore."

"I don't know if that's what it is, but I know I can't be with you anymore."

She reached across the table and caressed his hand. "Spend tonight with me."

"It wouldn't be right." He pulled away. "I'm sorry." He stood up to leave.

"Where are you going?"

"Better to make a clean break, for both of us, I think. Take care of yourself, Sandy."

Stanton left the restaurant and glanced back once when he was near the exit. She was looking down at the table, then she pulled out her cell phone. Stanton waited outside and watched through the glass. He saw her start to cry then hang up. He knew who was on the other end of that phone.

As Stanton rushed into Ransom's office, the secretary shouted that she was going to have him arrested. He stood in front of his desk, and Ransom looked up from the reports he was reading, peering at Stanton over his reading glasses.

"Let's talk," Stanton said.

"It's all right, Michelle," he told his secretary, who had followed Stanton into the office.

When the secretary left, Stanton sat down. He did a quick take of the unfamiliar office, noticing the bare walls. "What do you want with Sandra?"

"My relationship with Detective Porter is no concern of yours."

"What do you have over her? Is it drugs?"

"That, and some other things."

"What other things?"

"You're no longer a member of this department, remember? I can't just go around letting skeletons out of the closet on my detectives to the general public."

"She hasn't done anything wrong."

He grimaced. "How the hell would you know? Besides, what are you so worried about? You've got a wife and kids you're returning to."

"I want you to leave her alone."

"Or what, Jon? You gonna kill me, too?"

"No, I would never physically harm you. But everyone's got dirt. I still have a lot of friends here and in the media. And you know what I'm capable of when I want to find something. I'll find that dirt if I want to."

Ransom's face flushed red, the anger bubbling to the surface so quickly he could barely contain it. "Get the fuck outta my office."

Stanton stood and went to the door. "There's going to be a reckoning, Ransom. Wickedness can't hide forever."

36

Calvin sat in the sand at Ocean Beach Park and snacked on vegetables and flavored water. In high school, rather than going to class, he had spent his time at the beach or surfing. But the atmosphere was far different than he remembered.

Something about it was darker now. The fights and turf disputes that had taken place when he was younger were usually settled with fists. Then everybody went out for beers, and the loser bought the winner his drinks for the night.

Now, a fistfight could easily turn into a gunfight, and most of the surfers kept away from each other. Violence seemed about to erupt at any moment, and no one wanted to get too friendly with anyone who could be a potential enemy.

His cell phone rang, and the ID said Karen Lofgren was calling.

"Hey, Karen."

"Hi. They said you were sick. You doin' okay?"

"I'm fine. Just didn't feel like coming in today."

"Well, what're you doing?"

"Just hanging out on the beach."

"What beach?"

"OB."

"I'm off in ten. I'll be down."

"I'm not really—"

She hung up before he could finish. He put the phone down and scanned the beach again for the face he had memorized. No sign of him. Calvin had done a search for him on an investigative website and found his current address. This was the closest beach to his house that had decent waves.

He lay back on the sand, pulled his sunglasses down, and fell asleep.

Calvin woke a little later to a cold sensation running down his chest. He jumped up and grabbed the hand that was near him, twisting the wrist.

"Ow, Calvin! That hurts."

He flipped off his sunglasses and saw Karen holding a cold can of soda. He let go of her hand.

"Why would you do that?"

"Do what?"

"Don't ever surprise me, Karen."

"Someone took their asshole pills today." She sat down next to him. "That really hurt."

"I'm sorry. I didn't know it was you."

"Why didn't you answer my texts?"

"I was asleep."

She looked out over the water. "Well work was a pain in the ass. How was lying around on the beach all day?"

"Tough, but someone's gotta do it."

She turned to him and was smiling now. "So you gonna teach me how to surf or what?"

The day went by quickly, and the sun began to set too soon. Calvin had spent the entire time with Karen out on the open ocean. They had taken a break for a leisurely meal of hamburgers and fries at a shack nearby then had an afternoon nap on towels laid out over the hot sand.

They went out on the water one more time and paddled far from shore. They were alone, and the waves had died down. Calvin ran his fingers over the surface of the cool water.

"Hey, Calvin?"

"Yeah?" he said, watching the sunlight flicker off his fingers dipped into the sea.

"How come we never... I mean, it seems like you should'a asked me out by now."

"Asked you out? What are we, in *Leave it to Beaver?* You wanna go steady?"

"Don't be a prick. You know what I mean."

"Yeah. I don't know. How come you never asked me out?"

"'Cause that's not how you're supposed to do it."

"Oh, Ms. Feminism still likes the man to do all the work, huh?"

"It's just nice."

"Okay, well, Karen, would you like to go out with me tonight?"

She smiled and said, "Yes, Calvin, I would."

They paddled back to shore, and Calvin told her he would pick her up around nine. One of their mutual friends was having a party he could take her to. He got into his car and headed home.

As he came to a stop in front of his house, he checked his watch: 6:11 p.m. His father, who never came home before eight, wouldn't be there yet.

When Calvin walked in, his mother was waiting for him in the living room. She was sitting on the couch, her arms crossed, an open Bible next to her. "Where you been?"

"Work."

She grabbed the Bible and flung it at his face. He got his hands up in time, and it impacted his forearms.

"You lie to me, boy?"

"I'm not lying."

"Some whore from your work called here and asked where you were."

"I was at work, Mama," he said, looking at the floor.

"You was not at work." She jumped up and got in his face. "Were you with that whore that called? Answer me, boy. Were you with that whore?" She slapped him across the face. "Were you with that whore?"

"She's not a whore, Mama."

"Oh, excuse me. I'm sorry then that I called her one. That was inappropriate of me." She turned around then swung back, scraping the jewelry on her wrist across his face, cutting him. "You spendin' time with whores, and then you come to my house and lie to me? Wait till your father gets home. He's gonna deal with you. Now you go wait in the cellar for him."

"No," he whispered.

"What did you say?"

"I said no, Mama. I'm not goin'."

She grabbed his hair and pulled him down far enough that she could bash her fist against the back of his head. She picked up a nearby lamp and hit him in the head with it over and over, but it didn't break.

"No, Mama! Stop!"

She screamed and pounded the lamp against his head until it shattered. Calvin, dizzied and bleeding, came up with a hook that smacked her jaw and sent her flying into the wall.

His mother lay unconscious on the ground, moaning lightly as she stirred. He had felt her jaw against his fist, and he knew he'd broken it. His little brothers were watching from the hallway, and he looked at them and said, "Call Daddy to hurry home."

After calling an ambulance, Calvin left the house and shut the door behind him, tears streaming down his face. He opened the door again, thinking of his mama lying on the floor, hurt. When she woke up, she wouldn't want to see him. Despite everything, he still ran to her and turned her over. Her jaw hung limply, and her cheek was deep red.

"Mama, I'm sorry. Mama, please wake up. Wake up."

Calvin held her in his arms until the ambulance arrived. The paramedics loaded her onto a gurney and took her out. Her eyes were opening and closing, and the paramedics said she could have been having a seizure. Calvin jumped into the ambulance and rode with her to the hospital. She peered at him through eyes filled with hatred, but then she closed them. Her eyes didn't open again until they got to the ER.

He waited outside her room. Eventually, the doctor came out. A slim woman with a British accent, she had brunette hair peppered with gray. She placed a pen in her pocket before coming to stand in front of him.

"Are you a relative?"

"Son."

"Well, your mother is going to be fine. She took quite an impact, but there's no permanent damage. We thought the jaw might be broken, but the X-rays came back fine. She just needs some rest and ibuprofen for the swelling."

Calvin put his face in his hands, mostly to wipe the tears that wouldn't stop streaming. "Good, good." He rose. "I'm going to have my father come pick her up."

"So what happened to her exactly? She wouldn't say."

"I don't know. I came home and found her unconscious. She has epilepsy, and sometimes she falls."

"Huh. Well, regardless, she's going to be fine."

"Thanks."

Calvin left the hospital and sat on a bench just outside the emergency room exit. The wind was blowing through the leaves of nearby trees, and a plane flew by overhead. He listened to the rumble of its engines until they faded away to nothing. Then he rose and went to his car. There was only one place in the world he wanted to be right now.

As he drove along I-5, he pulled out his phone and dialed his father.

"Yeah."

"Hey, Daddy."

"What is it, Cal? I'm really busy right now."

"Mom's in the hospital."

"For what?"

"I think she fell. I don't know."

"Fell where?"

"At the house. Anyway, I told them that you would pick her up. I have to go on a date, and I can't do it."

"You have to go on a date rather than take care of your injured mother?"

"I just... I can't see her right now."

"What the hell are you talking about? Calvin, did you do something to your mother?"

"No."

"We talked about this, Cal. Do you remember? We talked about the dark urges."

"No, I didn't do that. I... I have to go."

His father continued to talk, but Calvin hung up the phone and threw it on the passenger seat. His tears were making his vision blurry. He wiped his eyes with the back of his arm.

Calvin drove past a dump and up a winding hill packed tightly with homes. The houses were decrepit, but the residents of this area were proud and rebellious. Tibetan flags hung on many porches, and Priuses were parked in a lot of driveways. Many of the neighborhood residents were college students, and many more were illegal immigrants. It was close to the Mexican border, and by and large, law enforcement left the people here alone.

He pulled into the underground parking lot of the apartment complex and parked in his stall. The lot had only fifteen other spaces, and only two were full. He got out and took the stairs to the third floor. The paint was chipping, and the carpets were stained beyond cleaning. But because most of the residents were illegal, the landlord left things alone. Rent of seventy-five dollars was due every week, and Calvin sent cash in the mail, along with a note indicating what apartment it was for. The landlord didn't even ask for ID to sign a lease since most residents wouldn't be able to produce one.

He unlocked the door to his apartment—number 355—and stepped inside. The air was stale, so he opened all the windows. He stood in the front room and let the breeze wash over him. The steel bars on the windows cast dark shadows across the floor, making him claustrophobic. He turned away from them and went to the kitchen. The surface of the large stainless steel table in the dining room area was polished to a shine with bleach, although the surrounding carpet was speckled with dark-black stains. Chain restraints dangled from each end of the table, and the toolbox in the corner held saws, knives, hammers, pliers, and a blowtorch. A car battery with small clips was underneath the table.

He pulled a Gatorade from the fridge, took several long swigs, then put the bottle back and went to the bathroom. He'd turned the room into a darkroom a week after renting the place, and he stood staring at himself in the mirror a long time before shutting the door.

He had grown accustomed to the dark. His mother had been locking him in the cellar since he was six months old, and he rarely knew anything else. The only thing he had been allowed to take down with him were dolls from a sister he barely knew. She had died of leukemia at twelve years old. He had reflections of her in his mind, but the last time he'd seen her had been so long ago that he couldn't tell if they were really memories of her or just the image of her he had created.

She had stood up to their mother on his behalf. She would yell and scream and threaten to call the police when his mother beat him. Sometimes his mother relented and went to drink herself to sleep. Sometimes she locked them both in the cellar for days at a time without food.

He remembered his sister's embrace in the dark, her warm flesh against his as they waited patiently for that door to open. They often talked about mundane things: how much they hated school and the people who teased and bullied them for their poor clothes or the holes in their shoes. They rarely spoke about why their father never helped them. They decided it was an unanswerable question.

Calvin flipped on the safelight, revealing the twenty or so photos hanging by small clips from the shower curtain rod. They showed a young blonde girl, spanning from photos of her outside to ones of her sitting in her classroom, which he'd taken with a zoom lens while standing across the street, to photos of her sleeping in her bed, the leaves from the tree in their yard visible on the periphery of the photo.

There was one taken from inside her house when her parents had forgotten to set the alarm. He had almost brought her to the apartment that night, but he'd decided against it. Impulsiveness was detrimental in his work, and he tried his best never to give in to it.

He took down one of the photos and stared at it a long time before replacing it. Soon, he wouldn't need these photos anymore because she would be here with him, and they would finally be together, as he knew they were meant to be.

37

Jonathan Stanton had left the force two days ago, and he had to admit to himself that he'd never felt better. His lawyer had called several times about prepping him for the deposition, but that had been moved out three weeks because Gary Coop had a family emergency, so the prepping could wait.

Stanton walked to the beach from his apartment and lay in the sand for a while before going out on the waves. They were decent but not large, and he rode them for a little over an hour then went back to the beach to wait for a better set.

He saw a young man struggling on his board off in the distance. The man continuously paddled out too far and came back too slowly. More than once, he fell off his board then sat in the water, hugging the board, trying to catch his breath. He finally got to shore then collapsed on the sand near Stanton.

"You're going out too far," Stanton said.

"I am?" he asked, out of breath.

"See where those guys are? That's about as far as you wanna go. And look how slowly they're paddling. You wanna save your strength. This isn't a race."

"Sure feels like it with how crazy you locals are." The boy got up, and Stanton noticed how muscular he was. "This is way harder than I thought it would be."

"How long have you been out here?"

"Today's my first day."

"Well you're gonna drown, you keep surfing like that. You need some lessons."

"Do you teach?"

"No. There's a rental shop over there that does daily lessons for cheap. The instructor's good, used to be a pro surfer in Hawaii."

"I don't know. Maybe I should quit. This doesn't seem like my thing."

"What you should ask yourself is why you want to do it in the first place. Then you can answer whether you should continue to do it."

He shrugged. "I'm new out here and just thought I'd try something new." He held out his hand. "Kyle James."

"Jon Stanton. Nice to meet you."

"You, too. So how long you been surfing?"

"Almost twenty years. Since I was in high school."

"No shit? That's crazy. I can't think of anything I've been doing for twenty years."

"The ocean's not like other things. You can fall in love with it. You'll start dreaming about it. Pretty soon, you won't be able to do anything else. You'll want to spend all your time out here."

"That sounds nice. Just the part about having something give your life meaning like that."

"I don't know about that, but the ocean's going to draw you in if you give it a chance. But first, you have to not die. You need lessons, Kyle."

"I don't really have any extra money for that, you know?"

"First lesson's free," Stanton said as he stood up. "At least take them up on that."

He turned toward his apartment, and Kyle followed him. He was awkward at carrying the board, and Stanton showed him how to tuck it under his arm so that he could keep both ends balanced. They walked to the parking lot, where Kyle had left his car.

"Hey, Jon, I really appreciate you takin' the time. Most of the guys out here won't even talk to me."

"You're an outsider right now, but they'll grow to you if you keep coming around."

"You gonna be here tomorrow, man?"

"Probably. Why?"

"Just thought maybe we could catch some waves together."

"I usually come in the early mornings."

He smiled. "All right, man. I'll see you then."

Stanton watched as Kyle threw the board on top of the car and tied it there with a stretchy cord. Kyle waved as he drove away, and Stanton thought he had seen his Volkswagen Beetle somewhere before.

38

The next morning, Stanton woke up late and sat on his balcony, where he read *Psychology Today* before opening a copy of *Fear and Trembling*. He read for hours, then went inside and napped before waking up around noon.

He hadn't felt this free since college. He could go anywhere or do anything, and nothing would stop him. He dreamed about flying off to Australia and living on the beach, surfing and eating crab and oysters by moonlight. He could go to Hawaii and live in a flat in the jungle, hike all day, and spend the nights surfing with friends.

He knew he would never do any of those things, though, because the thought of leaving his kids for even a short period filled him with dread. The world was a perilous place, and they needed him to look after them. When there was a bump in the night, Melissa called him, not 911. He was needed in San Diego in a way he wouldn't be anywhere else on earth. There was something about being needed that people craved, and he was no different.

He picked up his phone from the nightstand and saw he had three messages, all from Slim Jim. He called him back.

"Where the hell have you been?" Slim Jim answered.

"Sleeping."

"Pssh, you trying to make me jealous?"

"Yes."

"Well, it worked. Where are you?"

"Home."

"I'll be over in fifteen minutes."

"No, Jim, I—"

He hung up, and Stanton sat there a second before placing the phone back down and rising from his bed. He showered and changed into jeans and a University of Utah T-shirt then sat on the couch. He flipped channels on the TV, then settled on a tennis match, and he watched it until Slim Jim called from the lobby and told him to come down.

As he stepped off the elevator, he saw Slim Jim hitting on a woman in the lobby. Stanton leaned against the wall and waited until he was done. Toward the end of the conversation, the woman told him she had a boyfriend but said she'd enjoyed their talk. When she walked away, Stanton went over with a grin on his face.

"Was that as painful to watch as it was to do?" Slim Jim asked.

"Probably more so."

"She was hot. Kind of. I had to take a shot." He looked Stanton over. "No suit for Mr. GQ? This retirement thing is messing with your head."

"I've never felt better."

"Well, come have some of that good-feels rub off on me while we grab a pork burrito. You feel like a pork burrito?"

"Sure."

They got into Slim Jim's Corvette, and he drove to Señor Juan's Tacos. The interior was no bigger than an apartment and had only two tables and chairs, but the patio was large and packed with the lunch crowd. Slim Jim ordered two pork burritos and *horchatas* and brought them out to the table where Stanton was sitting.

"Love these damn things," Slim Jim said as he coated his burrito in ketchup. He took a large bite, and bits of brown pork dribbled out of his mouth. "How you liking no job?"

"I'm telling you honestly: I've never felt better. I don't know what it is, but I feel like a teenager again."

"Yeah," he said, wiping his mouth with a napkin, "yeah, that's the no-responsibilities bug. That's what my mom used to call it. She said it was a bug that would make you feel good for a minute and then screw you in the long run."

"Not sure that's true."

"I didn't believe it, either, but it is. You go without responsibilities or stress long enough, and you forget how to handle 'em. You get soft."

"I think I'll be all right, Jim."

"Maybe. But I won't be. They assigned the Sandman cases to me."

"I thought they closed the investigation?"

"Officially, yes. Unofficially, no. Could you imagine if there was another Sandman kidnapping? How much shit would the chief eat over that? They believed you—they didn't think Putnam was the right guy, either. They just wanted it handled right. If you would'a kept your mouth shut about it and just worked the cases, they wouldn't have said anything."

"I don't work that way."

"Nobody does, but you do it 'cause you have to. That's just the way the world works, young Padawan."

Stanton took a bite of his burrito. "Doesn't matter. I'm not a part of that anymore."

"Why? 'Cause you been on vacation for a week? You're a cop, Jon. You always will be. The only question is whether you're gonna wear the badge. Which brings me to the point of this little gathering. I need your help."

"With the Sandman cases?"

"With the Sandman cases."

"Jim, I'm—"

"Now wait a sec and hear me out. You're *the* guy on this case, Jon. You know it inside out. It would take me weeks to get up to speed. I need your help on this."

"I already quit."

"Pure consulting. Hell, I'll even pay you. But I need you on this. I can't work this case without your help."

He took another bite of the burrito, and ketchup dripped down his tie onto his shirt. He swore and dabbed at it with a napkin. Slim Jim was a pig, but he was sincere. If there was one thing cops didn't lack, it was ego, and for him to come with hat in hand, begging for help, was impressive.

"Let's say," Stanton said, "just for the sake of argument, that I agree to help. What would you want me to do?"

"Look at the evidence. There's no one better with evidence, and we both know it. Don't interview witnesses or anything. If you need to talk to a witness, you'll write your questions down, and I'll ask 'em."

He looked out over the intersection. A beige Cadillac with four male passengers was blaring bass-heavy music. Their arms, which were covered with prison tattoos, dangled out the windows. They had a menacing look about them, one that said they were actively looking for trouble. Many ex-cons couldn't adjust to life outside of prison and even committed crimes just to get back inside.

"I'll think about it."

"Come on, Jon. Don't do that to me. Yes or no, man? Come on. Don't leave me like that."

"Fine, yes, but only in a limited capacity. I'll look over some things and give you my opinion. I'm not invested in this, though."

"Of course. Just lookin' at the evidence."

"I can tell I'm going to regret this."

"This is who you are, man. Nothing to regret."

39

Stanton sat across from Kyle at the restaurant and ate coconut shrimp tacos with mango sauce. He'd been with Kyle for five days straight now. It wasn't even intentional; Kyle had stuck around each day until after Stanton was done surfing then asked him for a few minutes of lessons. Eventually, Stanton relented and took him out, showed him the type of equipment to get, how to get through the waves, and how to stand. Before long, Kyle was surfing well and could stay out for hours.

"It's a weird sport," Kyle said with a mouth full of food.

"Why?"

"You don't really do that much. The ocean does all the work."

Stanton grinned. "If you've realized that already, then it's too late. You've already fallen in love with it and will need to do it the rest of your life."

A pause in the conversation lasted long enough that Stanton noticed and knew Kyle had something to ask.

"Can I ask you something personal, Jon?"

"Yeah."

"Why'd your wife leave you?"

There was a slight sting in the question, but it didn't last long. Stanton took a drink of Diet Coke and let the question hang a moment before answering.

"It was mostly my job. She couldn't stand that I'd leave in the morning and she wasn't sure if I'd come home. On top of that, when I did come home, I could be moody and depressed."

"How come?"

"I see things I'm not sure people were meant to see day in and day out."

"Like what?"

"Mutilations, rapes, homicides… there's an ugly side to humanity that we all know about. But when you experience it every day, it begins to affect you. You don't look at people the same, 'cause you know they have a dark side that they don't share with anybody. You'll never know what it is, because some of the time, they don't even know what it is themselves. But it's there, and it's bigger than what we'd call their 'personality.' It controls them in a way they can't identify."

"So you'd have that dark side, too, then, wouldn't you?"

Before Stanton could answer, his phone rang. It was Taylor Rowe. "It's my lawyer, I gotta take this."

"No prob. I actually gotta get home. I'll see ya, Jon."

"Yeah." Stanton answered the phone as Kyle walked away. "This is Jon."

"Jon, it's Taylor Rowe."

"How's it going?"

"Not bad. How have you been holding up?"

"Okay."

"Well, I got some news. Coop's ready for the depo, and we got a date set in two weeks. When can you come by for some prep time?"

"What works with your schedule?"

"Today and tomorrow I'm open."

"Tomorrow works for me. I've got some things to catch up on today."

"Okay. Be by the office around ten. Shouldn't last more than a few hours."

"I might be a little late, but not by too much."

"That's fine. Just ask for me."

Stanton finished his meal and got into his car. On the passenger seat were copies of the files for the Sandman cases that Slim Jim had gotten him. The black-and-white photos were grainy, but all the same information was there. He picked up the file marked "Bethany Szleky" and flipped through the reports until he came to the information sheet. Her address was on the top right of the form, and Stanton memorized it then started his car.

40

The Szlekys lived just north of Balboa Park in the Hillcrest district. The neighborhood was known for its vibrant art scene and late-night parties at the local bars and clubs. Routinely, at the smaller bars that dotted the streets, owners locked the doors after closing time and continued with private gatherings until the sunrise.

In the eighties, it had been known as the winter district because of all the "snow"—the cocaine flooding in from Columbia and Mexico. Stanton remembered a girl he'd dated leaving for days at a time to party there. When she returned to the shack they shared with numerous other people, she'd sleep for days. Eventually, she disappeared, and he'd never found out what had happened to her.

The Szlekys lived in the Silver Crest Condominiums near a local fire station. Stanton pulled into the parking lot and admired the colorful buildings. Some were green, and others orange or red. It was monstrous—the mismatched colors bled into each other, but they were appealing somehow. *Youthful,* he decided.

At the south end was a building marked with a large *M*, and he walked to it and went downstairs to the second door. He knocked and rang the doorbell, but got no answer. Stanton waited another five minutes and tried again, but there was still no answer.

As he climbed the stairs to leave, two men carrying grocery bags came around the corner. Stanton passed them then turned as they walked to the second unit and began to unlock the door.

"Mr. Szleky?" he asked.

One of the men looked up. "Yes?"

"I'm Det—well... I'm working with the San Diego Police on your daughter's case. My name's Jon Stanton."

"Yes, of course. I remember you, Detective Stanton."

"Not anymore. I've actually retired. I'm just helping out with this case."

"What can I do for you?"

"To be honest, I'm not exactly sure. I'm just following up and was wondering if we could talk again."

"Come inside. Oh, this is my husband, James, by the way."

They nodded hello as Mark Szleky opened the door. Stanton followed them in and shut the door behind him. The condo was decorated tastefully and was immaculately clean. A white vase over the fireplace was filled with a leafy plant that was a vibrant crimson. Glass tables and black leather furniture stood on white carpet. It smelled faintly of men's cologne, and fitness magazines were spread on the coffee table.

"Have a seat."

Stanton sat down as the two men placed the groceries on the kitchen counter. Mark offered him a drink, but he declined. They sat across from him on the opposite couch and waited patiently for him to speak.

"You might've heard that there's been some confusion about whether we got the right person for Beth's disappearance."

"I saw the headlines."

He nodded. "I'm not going to sugarcoat it. Darrell Putnam may not have been the man who did this."

"But the other detective told me Putnam confessed."

"No, he never confessed. His mother gave the impression that he had said some things to her about the kidnappings, but when we grilled her and followed up, she admitted he never did."

"So you think the man who kidnapped Beth is still out there?"

"I honestly don't know."

James said, "Do you think Beth could still be alive? They keep calling this the Sandman Murders, but there's a chance she's still alive, right?"

"The chances are extremely remote. There's no evidence either way on this. I wish I could tell you something more positive, but I can't."

Mark took a deep breath, and James kissed him on the cheek.

"Beth was Mark's daughter from a previous marriage. Her mother committed suicide some time ago."

"I'm sorry to hear that."

Mark shrugged. "Everybody's got their demons. What is it we can do for you, Detective?"

"Please, call me Jon. And I just want to know if there was anything, anything at all, that we might've missed in the initial investigation. Did Beth have any friends we didn't follow up on, or are there some relatives we didn't speak with? A neighbor who seemed suspicious after the disappearance... anything?"

"I don't think so. Beth was kind of a loner. She had one friend, a girl named Kyra, who moved away to Florida, and I think you guys already spoke to her. You did a great job, Jon. We don't blame you for anything that's happened. Even if that son of a bitch Darrell Putnam wasn't the one who did this."

"I appreciate that. I wish I could do more, but I'm lost on this case. The three girls we thought were taken by Putnam have nothing in common. There's no thread connecting them."

"How do you know it was all one person then?"

"They were taken in the same area. They're about the same age, have similar hair and facial features. They were taken in the middle of the night by someone using a glass cutter. It's not coincidence—it's one person. Or two people working together."

Mark looked at the floor, anger filling his eyes. Stanton knew he had reopened a wound that was just barely starting to heal. He knew the images going through Mark's mind: the look of terror on Beth's face as she was woken by a man in her room, the horror of being dragged out to an awaiting car... the pain she probably felt before her death.

"I'm sorry, Mark. I shouldn't have—"

"No, no. It's… it's not you. I think about this so much, just never out in the open. It hurts."

James put his arm around Mark and pressed his forehead to his.

Stanton got the impression that he should probably leave. "I think that's all I needed for now. Do you mind if I just have one more look through her room?"

"Of course."

He rose and went down the hallway. In a large photo of Mark, James, and Beth at Disneyland in front of the Indiana Jones ride, they appeared carefree and happy. Stanton hoped that Mark could look at that photo and wipe away the images he'd conjured of her last night on earth.

He turned into the first bedroom. The room was exactly as he remembered it. Very few families of missing children changed anything in the child's room. It was a way of holding on, keeping some connection, no matter how loose, to the kids who had filled up their lives. It pained him each time he saw it.

Stanton heard soft sobbing in the living room, and he stepped into the room and shut the door. He sat on the edge of the bed, scanning the room. Forensics had been through here twice: once as part of the investigation and once more two weeks later as a favor to Stanton. His eyes would catch nothing that hadn't already been examined, but he looked anyway.

He opened the closet. The clothing inside had gathered dust, including the shoes that would never be worn by Beth again. He had no doubt that one day, far in the future, Mark would donate all these clothes to a charity, and they would be filled with the vibrancy of another child. But right now, they were gravestones, each and every article of clothing. He closed the closet and was about to leave when he spotted something on her dresser.

A shock went through his body, and he didn't trust himself to stand. He put his hand against the closet just to be sure. He closed his eyes and then opened them slowly, to ensure that what he was seeing was really there.

There was no doubt in his mind now: he was going to find who had taken Beth Szleky.

41

Calvin Riley sat on the couch while the party was going on around him. He wondered why he had allowed Karen to talk him into coming. The people here were in their late teens and early twenties, but Calvin felt as if he had absolutely nothing in common with them. They were beneath him. He was a tiger, and they were mice, unworthy even to be near him. But instead of knowing and accepting that knowledge, they pranced around, looking down their noses at him.

"Hey." Karen flopped down on the couch next to him, the smell of weed on her breath and clothes. "You having fun?"

"Not really."

"Have some pot." She held up a joint to his lips.

"No thanks."

"Why not?"

"My training."

She shrugged. "More for me."

Calvin pulled out his phone and saw that no one had called or texted. He had sent several texts to Stanton, hoping he could come over with a few beers tonight, and they could talk. Stanton had seemed distracted earlier, and Calvin wanted as much information as he could get about that.

"Make love to me." Karen wrapped her arms around his neck.

"What?"

"Make love to me," she said again, nibbling on his ear.

"Here?"

"No, silly. Take me home."

"Not tonight."

"Why not?"

"I just don't feel like it."

"But I do." She ran her tongue up his neck.

"Cut it out."

"What's wrong?"

He lifted her arms from his neck. "I said cut it out."

"What's the matter with you?"

"I just don't... feel that way about you. That's all."

She sat back on the couch and looked at him as if he had struck her. "You don't feel that way about me? Well, fuck you, Calvin Riley. You don't feel that way about anyone. I've never even seen you look at a woman. Are you gay or something?"

"No, I just don't want to have sex with you."

"Well, fuck you," she said louder as she stood up.

People at the party were beginning to take notice.

"You think you're so badass. You're not shit."

"I'm leaving."

"Fine, go. I could fuck any guy I want here."

"Then do it. Fuck them all."

She grabbed a beer can off a side table and flung it at him. It hit him in the face and fell to the floor. He looked up at her, and she took a step backward.

"You're going to regret doing that." He turned away and headed to the door.

"Calvin, wait. Calvin!"

As he stepped outside, he wiped the beer off his cheek and got to his car before Karen caught up to him. She grabbed his arm and tried to turn him around, but Calvin swung back with a fist and smashed it into her jaw. She fell back, and he crouched over her, squeezing her throat. She began to choke and cough, and he watched her, never taking his eyes away from hers... until he realized where he was.

He let go and stood up, the shock of what had happened overtaking him. He had to lean against his car just to keep himself upright.

How did I let that happen? How could I be so stupid after being so careful about everything else?

Karen was on the ground crying when a partygoer who'd witnessed it all from the porch went inside and came back with two other guys.

"What the fuck, bro?" one of them said. "You hittin' on bitches at my party?"

"I'm sorry... I—I wasn't... I'm just sorry. I'll leave."

"Fuck you, you'll leave. Bear, kick his ass."

The largest of the three ran over and swung with a right. Without even realizing fully that he was fighting, and with no fear or hesitation, Calvin ducked under the punch and delivered an uppercut into Bear's groin. Before Bear could respond, Calvin grabbed his genitals and twisted nearly all the way around, feeling a slight crack against his palms as one of the man's testicles burst. Bear screamed, and Calvin came up with an elbow into his throat that sent the big man to his knees.

The other two men didn't move. Calvin looked at them, and the one who owned the house held up his hands as if to surrender. Calvin grabbed the large one on his knees by the back of his head and thrust his thumbs into the man's eyes as far as they would go. Blood shot out, spurting over his shirt and down onto the driveway. He did a final twist of his fingers, and the man fainted from pain.

Calvin looked up and saw several more people watching from the porch. *I'm so stupid. How could I be so stupid?*

He turned and ran, leaving his car behind.

By the time Calvin slowed down and realized where he was, his heart felt as if it were pumping battery acid through him. He figured he had run five miles without a single stop. He sat down on a nearby bus bench and looked up at the moon, feeling its light over him, letting it fill his body.

He had been so careful for so long that it felt routine, but something had been changing the past year. He had been forgetting things, speaking to people he shouldn't have spoken to, going places he shouldn't have gone. He had even ended up at a cop bar one night, drinking with a bunch of patrol cops, talking about the cases he had perpetrated. He was so stupid—he knew that now. He had known arrogance was dangerous, and he had become too arrogant.

The man back at the party would survive, but Calvin could be charged with felony mayhem or even attempted murder. He could be looking at prison. Calvin struck himself in the face. *How could you be so stupid?*

A thought danced into his head: his car was back at the party. His name was on the registration card. It wouldn't matter anyway because Karen would tell everyone his name. And if they went to his house... *What's at the house?* He racked his brain, trying to remember if he had left anything there. *What would they find? A piece of clothing? A ring?* He couldn't remember what was there.

They would never find the apartment.

Or did I jot the number down on something at the house?

He hadn't memorized the address at first; he'd written it down.

Where?

Calvin stood and hurried down the sidewalk, mumbling to himself, going through the lists of items he knew he had at his house. He pictured his room and went through it, naming each item aloud.

The pressure was too much for him. He needed his father. His father would help him out of this, but first, he needed time to think and calm down. He took out his phone and called Stanton. There was no answer, so he left a message.

"Hey, Jon, this is Kyle. Can you call me back? I kinda need a place to stay for a couple days. I got evicted 'cause of money stuff. Anyway, can you please call me back? I'm gonna be waiting for your call."

He hung up and headed toward a diner down the street, intending to wait there. Though Stanton hadn't known him long, he didn't strike him as someone who would turn away another person when he could help. Stanton would help him.

42

Stanton stood outside the Szlekys' condo and called Slim Jim. The photo of Beth was still in his hand; her father had given him permission to take it.

Slim Jim answered on the third ring. "Yeah, Jon, what's up?"

"Run a check of the three girls' sports teams."

"What?"

"Yvette, Sarah, and Beth all played sports. Either softball or soccer."

"You think it's someone involved on their teams?"

"No, run a check of who did their photos. They all had similar photos. We need to cross-reference all the names involved with the team photos. All the photographers, assistants, secretaries, and then if nothing hits on all three, we need to see where the photos were developed and do the same thing there."

"You think that's really it?"

"I know it, Jim. This is the connection. This is what all three have in common. We're gonna get this guy… Jim, you still there?"

Stanton heard a familiar sound off in the distance. He wouldn't have noticed, but Slim Jim stopped speaking when he heard them through the phone. They were sirens.

"What was that?" Stanton asked.

"What?"

"You stopped speaking when you heard the sirens."

"Jon, you need to know something. I didn't have a choice."

"Choice for what? What did you do, Jim?"

"I'm sorry."

The sirens grew closer and rounded the block. Stanton realized they were coming for him. "What'd they give you, Jim? What'd they give you to sell me out?"

"It's not like that."

The patrol cars screeched to a halt in front of the condos, and two officers jumped out. Behind them was another unit, and one of the officers stepped out with a shotgun. They took aim and demanded he get down on the ground and put his hands behind his head.

Stanton dropped his phone and did what they wanted.

The cell was cold though the temperature outside was nearly eighty degrees. Stanton sat on a cot next to a steel toilet and sink that appeared new. In fact, this cell was never used anymore. In the back of the precinct, it had only been used temporarily, years ago when they'd needed a place to hold the inmates during renovations.

No one else was nearby, and the door leading to the rest of the precinct was locked. He stood up and paced the cell for a while, but he quickly grew bored and lay down on the cement floor, staring up at the harsh lights. He put his hands behind his head and closed his eyes. He pictured himself on the beach, lying on his back in the soft sand, listening to the laughter of people playing in the water.

Stanton heard the door open but didn't respond. He heard a chair brought near the cell and the slow, deliberate breathing of the person sitting there. Stanton eased himself out of his mind's eye and returned to where he was. He looked over and saw Ransom Talano sitting backward on a folding chair.

"Do you want something to eat?"

"I'm fine. Thank you."

"You sure? You may be in here a while."

Stanton sat up.

"Do you know why you're here?" Ransom asked.

"Yes."

"Then you know what I'm going to be charging you with."

"My guess would be impersonating an officer and obstruction of justice."

"I had just thought about the obstruction, but the impersonating charge's brilliant. That was what you were doing, you know, acting like a cop when you weren't one. That's what you've been doing a long time now, isn't it?"

"Who exactly is it that you think I am?"

"I think you're Harlow. And Eli Sherman. And Meadgers and Rogers and Rojas and the whole damned lot of 'em."

"I'm not. I testified against Harlow. I was the one who provided everything to the feds. I did everything I could to stop him."

"And how many Nazis said the same thing after the war? It's easy to look back and say you did everything you could. It's much harder to actually help."

"What did you expect me to do?"

"I expected you to stop them. To come to IAD with your information and wear a wire. To bring those sonsabitches down."

"I didn't know if his reach extended to IAD or not. I couldn't trust you."

"Bullshit. You can't trust yourself because you don't know what you want. That's how it works: you figure out what you want, see it in your mind, and then work to it. You didn't know if you wanted to bust your pal Harlow or not. Granted, you were in a tough fucking spot. But you made a choice and crapped out. Now it's time to pay the piper."

"What you did was entrapment. I'll beat it."

"I know. But you'll spend some time in jail and be in all the papers. You won't even be able to find a job as a security guard after this is all done."

"I've already quit. I don't think that's it. There's something else with you. Something driving you. This is personal, not professional."

Ransom stood and moved the chair back against the wall.

"Your bail's been set. I'm sure you can get someone in here to post it. If you've got anyone left."

43

Stanton spent another two hours in the cell before a uniform came to tell him bail had been posted. He gathered his wallet, belt, and keys from the front desk then walked out, expecting to see Melissa standing there. Instead, Sandra was leaning against her car, smoking.

"What are you doing here?" he asked.

"Something I never thought I would." She threw the cigarette on the ground and stepped on it. "Do you need a ride home?"

"I need to get my car out of impound, but I can just call a cab for now."

"I posted three grand for your bail. I think that's worth a conversation."

Stanton nodded and got into the passenger seat. As they pulled away, Sandra lit a fresh cigarette and rolled down her window. "I can't believe I let this happen to you."

"What do they have on you, Sandy? It wasn't just drugs. Lots of cops are strung out. What is it? No lies."

She took a few long draws from her cigarette then knocked the ashes out the window. She waited until they came to a stoplight to start speaking again. "I was fresh out of the academy, not even a year. They needed girls to volunteer for some busts the county was doing with the LAPD. There was a meth house run by some white supremacists, the White Reich, a prison gang out of the Midwest that made their way here. I was under almost six months. I did things they never trained me for. They made me strip for them once, and I had to make out with another girl.

They were going to gang rape me, but I got out of it by telling them I was infected with AIDS. You have to say AIDS because if you say gonorrhea or genital warts or anything like that, they won't care. They'll still rape you. That was one thing I learned from the other girls who were there.

"After about six months of hanging out with them, they trusted me enough to keep me around when they were packaging their drugs. I got a lotta good stuff. Distribution channels, profits—we even found out they had a judge on their payroll. Everything was going good. But some fucking rookie cop that I was at the academy with saw me and came up to say hi. I pretended like I didn't know him, and everything seemed fine. I wasn't experienced enough yet to know that they kill people they even suspect of working with the cops.

"When we got to the house that night, two guys grabbed me and dragged me into a room. They smacked me around and took off their clothes. They said they were going to call everyone they knew to come over and rape me, and when they got a piece, they were going to take me to a field and light me on fire. That's what they did to people who worked with the cops. But the room they put me in was where I slept most nights. I kept a gun under the bed. They threw me on the floor, and I went for it and got it. I put a slug into the first one's head, and the other one tried to jump on top of me and got three into his chest. He died right there, on top of me. I saw his face as he died.

"I was scared, Jon. I was new, and I didn't know what was going to happen. One of the other girls—the one who told me about the AIDS thing—she ran into the room when she heard the shots. She hadn't heard that I was suspected of being a cop. She thought the two guys were just going to rape me, and I'd shot them. She took the gun from me and told me to get out of there and never come back."

"What'd you do?"

"I left. When I went in to the station, I thought they could charge me with murder. So I didn't say anything. I just said that there'd been a fight and two guys had shot each other. They thought I was a cop because I'd tried to stop them, so I couldn't go back. I knew none of those guys would talk, so no one would ever find out what really happened. They sent some patrols to check out my story, but when they got to the house, the bodies were gone, and no one would talk.

She sighed and waited a few beats before speaking again.

"So after that, I transferred from L.A. to San Diego, and I thought it was over. Then I got a box in the mail. It was from Ransom. It was the gun I had used to shoot those men. I don't know where he found it or how, but he did. He called me the next day and said that he wasn't going to tell anybody, but that I would have to do some work for him now."

"You didn't do anything wrong. Deadly force was justified."

"Who would believe me now? It would be IAD doing the investigation. Do you really think they would believe me? If Ransom knows where the bodies are, they will charge me with murder, Jon."

Stanton looked out the window. They were passing a homeless shelter, and the line for food stretched around the building and down the sidewalk. There were several families with children standing in line next to meth-heads and the insane.

"He needs to be stopped," he said.

"How?"

"I don't know. But I think there's one person who might."

44

The Federal Correctional Institution in Lompoc, California, had a special building on the prison grounds used to house minimum-security inmates. As the cab dropped Stanton off at six in the morning in front of the facility, the guards were just going through their morning ritual of waking everybody up and getting ready for breakfast hour.

Sandra had called ahead and used her detective credentials to set an appointment for him. He had given her specific instructions to carry out while he was gone: run a crosscheck of every person associated with the team photos of the victims in the Sandman cases. Sandra had reluctantly agreed after he told her he couldn't turn to anyone else.

Stanton went inside the white rectangular building with the blue metal awning over the front entrance. He fiddled absently with the lighter in his pocket a few minutes before taking a deep breath and walking to the reception area. He checked in and got a locker to hold his wallet, lighter, and keys. The clerk gave him a visitor's badge. He sat for twenty minutes in the waiting area before a correctional officer came and led him to the inmate visiting area.

He was surprised how different a minimum security federal facility was from a state prison. The state prison was stained cement and metal stools. The federal facility was couches and coffee tables—there was even a vending machine.

Michael R. Harlow came out in his prison jumpsuit. Harlow waited until the guard was at the other end of the hall before speaking.

"I dreamed about this moment, but I never thought it would happen."

"I have something to talk to you about, Mike. So say what you need to say so we can get to it."

Harlow sat down across from Stanton in a recliner. "Say what I'm going to say? I'm going to spend the rest of my life in here because of you."

"No, Mike. You're going to spend the rest of your life in here because of you."

There was a long pause as the two men stared at each other.

"You know, the guard's not paying attention. I could probably snap your neck before he even looks in this direction. I got nothing to lose."

"That's not true. You'd get transferred away from all your minimum-security white-collar buddies and be put in gen pop at the federal pen. You'd be a former chief of police serving with high-level drug dealers, rapists, and gang bangers. I hear they let you play golf in minimum security. Is that true?"

Stanton watched Harlow crumble before his eyes. His posture went from proud and defiant to weak and pathetic.

He slouched on the chair and took a deep breath. "What do you want, Jon? Did you just come here to see me like this?"

"I take no pleasure in your suffering. I never wanted this."

"I know you didn't. You gave me a chance to turn myself in. That's what that was, wasn't it? I could'a told 'em the story from my side of things."

"To be honest, you were my friend. I was kinda hoping you would run to Mexico and we would never see you again."

Harlow grinned. "I've gotten to know everybody in here, and you know what I've realized? It wouldn't matter. When you do evil, evil has a way of coming back on you. Weird as hell, but it's true."

"I've never thought otherwise." Stanton cleared his throat nervously. He thought he'd lost that particular nervous tic. "Mike, there's a reason I'm here. I need to ask you for something."

"This ought to be good. What is it?"

"You read the news about what's going on?"

"Yeah, I know about the suit and all that. What is it exactly you need help with?"

"Ransom Talano from IAD. He wants to destroy me and every other detective who ever happened to be working when you were chief."

Harlow shook his head. "I hated that guy. You know I was the stupid bastard who actually promoted him from detective to IAD?"

"It's more than an investigation for him. It's personal. He's obsessed with me. He even showed up at my house."

Harlow leaned forward. "I know, deep down, it's my fault I'm in here. But part of me still wants to jump over this table and strangle the life out of you, Jon. I can't help you."

"You can't, or you won't?"

"I won't."

"What if I were to give you something in exchange?"

"What could you possibly have that I would need in here?"

"Your wife will eventually get remarried, but there'll still be things you need. She'll do those things for a while, but she'll find it a hassle and realize she doesn't see you that much anyway. You'll need someone to do those things for you."

"And what things would those be?"

"I have no idea. But things will come up. Maybe you'll need to talk to your son about sex or drugs, and he won't come here. I could take what you want to tell him down to him. Or maybe bring you information on whoever your wife marries. Stepdads can easily be abusers, Mike. You're going to want someone keeping an eye on that. Or maybe you just want some books or types of food you can't get in here."

Harlow looked back at the officer, who glanced at them then turned and walked in the other direction again.

"How do I know you'll keep your word?" Harlow asked.

"You don't. But you know me. Do you think I won't?"

"No, I don't think that."

"Then help me beat this, and I'll help you. You know I'm right—you'll need things, and eventually, there won't be anyone else."

Harlow thought a long while, rubbing his face and looking at the lights on the vending machine.

"Ransom won't destroy you. Not until you're useless to him. I saw him take people to the brink, where they thought they couldn't make it, and then pull them back. But you owe him after that. That's what he wants: people he can control. You're no good to him as a civilian. He won't toss you from the force if he can help it."

"I already quit."

"No, don't quit. Get your job back. You're in the middle of a lawsuit. It doesn't look good for you to quit or be let go. Talk to Chin. I'm sure he'll give you your job back. IAD will have jurisdiction over you again, but I'm telling you, that's why Ransom won't go all the way on this."

"Then what?"

"Then you gotta dig up his skeletons before he digs up yours. And I've known that nasty fucker a long time, Jon. He's got a lot of skeletons."

45

Stanton sat on the balcony of his apartment, watching the ocean. His badge and gun lay on the side table next to him. He was amazed how simple getting them back had been. After one phone call to Chin Ho and signing a few papers, he was back on the force, though he was technically suspended with pay for two more days.

Harlow had been right: losing him in the middle of a lawsuit didn't look good. Ho had given him his job back too quickly, relief and desperation in his voice. Stanton had no doubt that after the lawsuit was settled, he would have hell to pay, but for now, he was a cop again.

Stanton picked up his phone and tried Kyle. He had left several messages saying he needed Stanton's help, but he never answered when Stanton returned those calls.

He was an odd man. He was too forward, too forceful about wanting to be friends. Stanton read a loneliness in him that instantly made him sympathize. Finding people to connect with in this world was difficult, and Stanton couldn't turn away someone who felt he didn't have anywhere else to turn.

There was a knock at the door, and Stanton waited until he heard it again to answer. The young kids in the condo complex sometimes knocked on doors then ran off. He opened the door to find Kyle standing there. He looked pale, as if he hadn't slept in a while, and his clothes were wrinkled and stained.

"Hey, Jon."

"I got your messages. What's going on?"

"Can I come in?"

"Yeah."

They sat on the couch.

"What's going on?" Stanton asked again.

"I got into some trouble, and I needed your help. But I took care of it."

"What kind of trouble?"

"It was at some stupid fucking party I never should'a gone to. But I took care of it, Jon. I took care of it."

Stanton could smell the potent odor of alcohol and marijuana emanating from him.

"Took care of it how?"

Kyle folded his arms. Stanton noticed the young man making a swaying motion, and he wasn't looking Stanton in the eyes.

"You got anything to eat? I haven't eaten yet today."

"Cold pizza okay?"

"That would be great."

Stanton put the pizza on a plate and brought it out with a glass of orange juice. Kyle attacked it with zeal, and Stanton waited quietly until he was ready to talk.

"So what's going on, Kyle? You don't seem like yourself."

"Don't I? I feel good. Better than I have in a long time."

"What was the trouble you were in?"

"I got into a fight at a party and hurt the guy pretty bad. But everything turned out okay. The only person who knew me there isn't going to say anything."

"Why'd you get into a fight?"

"Wasn't my choice," he said with his mouth full. "Hey, so what happened to that thing you were telling me about? That court thing?"

"The deposition?"

"Yeah, did it happen yet?"

"No, tomorrow morning. I spent all day today at my lawyer's office, preparing for it."

"Oh yeah? What're you gonna say?"

"The truth. I haven't done anything wrong, so I don't have

anything to be afraid of."

"But like you were saying, you think someone else was the Sandman. You can't, like, investigate that anymore, right? It's over. So aren't they gonna ask you about that?"

"They can ask whatever they want. I've got nothing to hide." Stanton leaned forward on his elbows. "I have an odd request, Kyle. And before you say no, I'd like you to hear me out."

"Sure, anything for you."

"I want you to come to church with me on Sunday."

Kyle sat there frozen a moment, then he burst out laughing. "You're kidding."

"No, I think you would really enjoy it. Religion has so much to offer. It can give you peace and comfort when you can't find it anywhere else. Just come with me once, and if you don't like it, I won't ask you again."

Kyle shrugged. "Sure, why not." He gulped his orange juice then wiped his lips on his arm before standing up. "I gotta go. My mom's expecting me."

"I didn't know both your parents lived here."

"Yeah, well, I don't talk about 'em much. I'll see ya later."

Stanton walked him out and watched him go down the hall to the elevator. He couldn't help but get the distinct impression that he was lost, a soul wandering around looking for anywhere to settle. He hoped God would be that place for Kyle James.

46

Smiling, Gary Coop sat across from Stanton, who was dressed in a white shirt with red tie, shiny black loafers to match. Coop thought he looked like a private investigator from one of those old 1930s black-and-white films he and his dad used to watch together.

Sitting next to Stanton, Taylor Rowe scribbled preparatory notes on a legal pad. Coop had always been attracted to Rowe. Something about the way she dressed and carried herself screamed Naughty Librarian. He had asked her out once, and she'd declined.

"Are you ready, Detective? Ah, it is Detective again, isn't it?"

"Yes."

"Okay, we on the record?" he said to the court reporter, who nodded. "All right. Please state your name and address for the record."

"Jonathan Stanton, 42 Ocean Beach Park, San Diego, California."

"And what do you do, sir?"

"I'm a detective with the San Diego Police Department in the Sex Crimes Division."

"How long have you been with the SDPD?"

"Twelve years."

Coop hesitated a moment. "Are you familiar with what has been termed the 'Sandman Murders'?"

"Yes."

"What are they?"

"Last year, between April and August, we investigated a

series of kidnappings within a short distance from each other. There were three of them: Yvette Reynolds, Sarah Henroid, and Beth Szleky."

"Kidnappings, not murders?"

"No, they were termed the Sandman Murders by some blogger and the term stuck. There's no evidence the girls were murdered."

"And why were they grouped together, Detective?"

"We believed they were committed by the same person."

"Why?"

"There were lots of similarities in the cases. All the girls were similar ages, between nine and twelve. They all had similar hair and comparable body types. They were taken from their homes between ten and two. The perpetrator used a glass cutter in all three cases to gain entry into the home. It was always the bedroom windows of the girls."

"Did you find any of the girls?"

"No."

"Did you find remains for any of the girls?"

"No."

"Then why let them continue to be called murders?"

Stanton shifted in his seat. "A huge number of child abductions, upward of ninety percent, are murders. It is very unlikely the girls are still alive after this long."

"Any items of clothing, jewelry, a note, a phone call, anything like that found or received?"

"No, nothing."

"So you had nothing from the case, no evidence, but you identified a suspect, isn't that true?"

"I wouldn't say we had no evidence. As I said, the crimes were nearly identical. You can also extrapolate from the methods used in the abductions. The perpetrator knew which bedroom was the victim's. That meant he watched the houses beforehand. It had to have been someone who wouldn't stand out in a predominantly white, upper-middle-class neighborhood. We could assume he was white from that. Most pedophiles of this type tend to stick within their own races, as well, and all the girls were white."

"So you guessed he was white. What else did you guess about him?"

"He had to have a car and be reasonably physically fit. One of the girl's rooms was on the second floor, and he climbed up and then back down with her."

"Couldn't there have been two of them doing the work?"

Stanton shrugged. "Yeah, and we never ruled that out. But there was only one set of shoeprints found in the Reynolds' garden underneath their daughter's window. If there was a second person, he would just have been the driver."

"So he's white and works out. Anything else?"

"He likely lived nearby, as well. He fit into the donut model of the crimes."

"What's the donut model?"

"Most offenders of this type commit crimes away from their homes to try to throw off the police. If they commit the crimes in enough locations, a pattern emerges. All of the locations end up being nearly identical distances from a few locations. Sometimes only one. That location is their home or their neighborhood—or their city if they operate statewide. If you get all the locations of the crimes up on a map and connect them, the pattern resembles a circle. The perpetrator's home or city is in the middle, like the center of a donut."

"Interesting theory. Is there any research to back that up?"

"I couldn't quote it off the top of my head, but I'm sure—"

"So the answer's no, as far as you know?"

"I suppose so, though I know a criminologist at UCLA was working on the theory."

"Now, did you have anything else that you were assuming about the perpetrator of these crimes?"

"No, other than he may have had some burglaries or voyeurism charges on his record."

"And why do you say that?"

"Most sex offenders, especially ones who move to kidnappings within homes, begin as burglars. One night, they find someone home and sexually assault them and then—"

"Is there any evidence in this case that any of the victims were sexually assaulted?"

"No."

"So it's another guess?"

"I suppose you could call it that."

"Now based on these guesses, you identified somebody as a suspect. Is that correct?"

"Yes."

"And who was that person?"

"Darrell Putnam."

"And it's true that you didn't have any direct evidence linking Mr. Putnam to any of these crimes?"

"Direct evidence? If you mean a note from him saying 'I did it,' then no, we didn't have that."

"What did you have?"

"He was a registered sex offender living within a few miles of each of the victims."

"So did you confront him about these allegations you made?"

"I wouldn't say *confront*. That's not the right word. We followed him for a few days, and then I came to his house to talk to him."

"Who followed him?"

"We had a unit from Sex Crimes trail him."

"And what did they find? Did they find anything linking this man to any of the crimes? Did they hear him utter a single word about these kidnappings?"

"No, they did not."

Coop took a note on the legal pad in front of him, a smirk on his face. "And so your surveillance turned up nothing, and you went over to his house. Is that right?"

"Yes."

"Tell me what happened when you went to his house."

"It was an older house, where he lived with his mother. I

parked my car in front of the house, and instantly one of the neighbors was out, asking me what I was doing there. I explained that I was a police officer and that he should go back inside. That I was just following up on a few things.

"When I got to the door, Darrell's mother came out. We talked for a few minutes about Darrell. I asked her if he was home, and the first thing she said was, 'What did he do now? He didn't hurt no kids, did he?'"

"Let me stop you there, Detective. I'm going to object to that and ask that it be stricken from the record as hearsay."

"Hearsay, my ass," Rowe responded. "You opened the door and asked it. We'll run a motion in limine with the judge about it later. Move on, Gary."

"Just to note for the record—I don't appreciate the use of your language, Ms. Rowe."

"You didn't mind it when you asked me out on a date a couple months ago knowing I was in a relationship."

Coop shifted in his seat. "So you meet his mom… then what happens?"

"She says he's up in his room, so I went into the house."

"Is that procedure?"

"What do you mean?"

"You're about to confront a man suspected of three child kidnappings. Is that procedure to go alone into his house?"

"I probably should've called for backup."

"But you didn't."

"No, I didn't. As I said, I was just there to talk. At this point, he wasn't even really a suspect, more a person of interest. I just wanted to see what he had to say about the whole thing."

"So you made a mistake?"

"No, I don't think I violated procedure because he wasn't a suspect."

"And what did he say when you confronted him?"

"I didn't get the chance. When I got up to his room, the window was open, and I saw him running across the backyard."

"What did you do?"

"I sprinted out of the house and called dispatch on my phone. We ran through his yard, and I hopped a fence after him. He got to the curb, where there was a car. He jumped in and took off, and I had to run back to my car to keep up with him. I caught up somewhere down the block and had to chase him down the freeway to downtown. He got cut off by a group of motorcyclists down by One American Plaza."

"What happened then?"

"I jumped out of my car because he was running by the time I got there. He headed into the building, and I went after him. I caught up to him on the roof—"

"How'd you know he was going to the roof?"

"The security guard station had cameras on all the elevators. I went over there and had them track him. Then I followed."

"So you're riding the elevator up to the roof. Was your firearm out at this point?"

"No."

"Where was it?"

"Holstered to my side."

"When did it come out?"

"When I got to the roof, Darrell was standing around. I don't think he expected me to find him so fast. He ran to the edge of the building and looked down like he was going to jump, and then he reached behind him. That's when I pulled it. I thought he might be reaching for a weapon."

"Did you see a weapon?"

"No."

"In fact, he didn't have a weapon on him. Is that correct?"

"Unless it got lost on the way down, no, he didn't have a weapon."

"So you pull out your firearm on a weaponless 'person of interest,' and then what?"

"I told him that he needed to turn himself in. He told me he knew what this was about and that he was innocent. I said if that was the case, then he would be cleared and free to go. Then he jumped."

"How did he jump?"

"He looked over the edge and then fell backward."

"Did you startle him?"

"No."

"Did you intimidate him?"

"No."

"Would you say it's reasonable to assume that if someone has a gun pointed at your head and you're standing on a ledge that you might be intimidated?"

"I suppose. But that wasn't my intent."

"Was your intent to have him fly off that roof?"

"Absolutely not."

"Okay, well, let me stop there for a second." Coop turned to the stenographer. "I need to run out to the restroom for about half a minute."

"Coop," Rowe said, "I know this trick." She turned to Stanton. "He wants us to talk while he's gone and then attorney-client privilege doesn't apply because there are other people in the room. He can get us to reveal what was said between us."

"No," Coop said, "I just gotta piss. You wanna come with me?"

"For the record, I don't appreciate your language."

Stanton's phone buzzed. Stanton looked down, and his face changed. He looked at Rowe. "I need to leave."

"What?" Rowe said. "You can't leave. We're in the middle—"

Stanton rose and began to walk out. "Reschedule. I'm really sorry, but I have to go."

Coop watched him walk out, then he turned back to Rowe. The stenographer had turned off the record and was packing up.

"Thought you had to piss," Rowe said.

Coop shrugged and took another sip of water. "I want him back as soon as possible. I'm not done with him yet."

Stanton raced down the freeway but came to a standstill near an accident. He got over past the white line and held up his badge to the officers handling the scene, and they let him pass. He shot down the nearest exit and over to the Northern Precinct.

He ran straight to the ready room, where Childs, Sandra, and Slim Jim were standing over documents and photos. Slim Jim glanced at him then away.

"Heard you're back from the dead," Childs said.

"For now. I got the text. What'd we get?"

Childs lifted a folder and laid photos of Yvette, Sarah, and Beth on the table. Then he pushed another photo toward Stanton: a snapshot of a storefront.

"Sandra followed up on your lead and then brought me in. Looks like you were right, Detective Stanton. There's an association with all three vics: Taylor Drugs."

47

Calvin Riley finished his sandwich and threw the wrapper away into the trash bin. Jersey Subs was the closest sandwich shop to his work, but their chicken was always too soggy. He went to the front counter and complained to the manager, who said all he could do was issue a refund. Calvin let him keep the money but said he wanted the chicken grilled next time.

As he got into his car, he smiled. He hadn't felt this good in a long time. There was something to being efficacious that brought him a sense of fulfillment. He had taken care of his business without the help of his father or Stanton. He felt like a real man, the type he'd seen in movies.

He drove to work and was about to pass the front entrance to go to employee parking when he saw two police cruisers out front. He stopped, his heart sinking in his chest, and looked through the glass. There was a lot of activity inside the store, and his manager was speaking with a few people, probably about Karen. She had been missing a few days and had not called into work.

Then, he saw Stanton's face. Stanton worked sex crimes; he wouldn't be here for a missing person. He was here for him.

Calvin felt vomit rise in his throat, and before he could stop it, bile spewed over the window and the driver-side door.

He pulled out of the parking lot and sped down the road until he came to a small park near a cluster of old factory buildings. He got out and ran to the bathroom. It stunk of piss and feces, and he puked over the sink and mirror.

When he was through, he sucked down water from the faucet then looked at himself in the mirror. *How did they find me? How could I be so careless?* He could think of only one explanation: Jon Stanton had found him. Jon Stanton was a demon. Calvin knew he should've killed him as soon as Stanton had let his guard down and allowed him into his home. He'd had the gun tucked away in the small of his back. He should've put a few rounds into Stanton's head when he had the chance.

Calvin stepped out of the bathroom and had to lean against the building. Everything seemed blurry, as though it had an edge of white around it, and he couldn't breathe. His chest hurt, and his hands felt numb. He held them up in front of his face, and they seemed like someone else's hands.

"Hey, asshole, you got some cash?"

Calvin turned to the voice. He was young with tattoos on his neck and hands. A cigarette dangled from his mouth.

"I'm talkin' to you. You got some cash?"

"No," Calvin mumbled.

The man watched him, sensing something was wrong. "What's the matter with you?" He waited a few seconds, and when he didn't receive a response, he walked to Calvin and began going through his pockets. Without resisting, he watched the man with detached curiosity, like someone watching an animal at the zoo.

In a single motion, he pulled out the hunting knife strapped to his leg and ran it across the man's throat. Warm blood spattered over him, and the man choked and wheezed. He fell to his back in front of the toilet. Calvin leaned over him and watched him die, looking into his eyes.

He put away the knife and headed to his car. Jon Stanton was too dangerous. The only way to get out of this was to barrel through him.

48

Stanton stood inside Taylor Drugs, looking at a display for lotion. It had been organized based on color, and in the middle was a single bottle out of sync with the rest. Stanton resisted the urge to put it back in its place and instead read the sign next to the display.

"Detective," the manager said as he stepped out from the back room, "I have the list you wanted."

Stanton and Childs went over to the counter as the manager pulled out a spreadsheet of all the employees.

"Okay," the manager said. "What are you looking for?"

"White male, late twenties or early thirties."

"Um, well you should probably talk to Spencer over there first." The manager pointed at an overweight man pushing a mop.

"No, he would be physically fit. Probably not in any sort of relationship or very social. But he might be a meticulous employee."

The manager went through the list, mumbling to himself and occasionally shaking his head as he crossed off names. "There's only two I can think of who are like that: Wes Bell and Calvin Riley."

"I need their contact information immediately. If you hear from them, you need to tell them that there's a glitch in their payroll paperwork, and you need them to come in and sign some new tax forms."

"Okay, okay, hold on. I'll get you that information."

Stanton turned to Childs, who had his arms folded and a grin on his face.

"You live for this shit, huh?" Childs said.

"Danny, I never thought that—"

"No need, brother. I don't believe a word them IAD shits are saying. You ain't got to explain anything to me. But I'm sorry, man. I'm sorry I didn't believe you. I should'a had your back."

The manager came out and handed them a computer printout listing addresses and phone numbers for the two men. "Do you need anything else, Detective?"

"No, that's it for now. Thank you. Just make sure not to act out of the ordinary if they come in. This man is going to be extremely dangerous when he's cornered."

"I can't imagine either of them that way. I wish Karen was here. She would tell you, too. She was dating Calvin."

"Where is she?"

"I don't know. She hasn't come into work this week. I tried calling, but her roommate doesn't know where she is, either."

Stanton looked at Childs then back at the manager. "I need her address, too."

After getting what they needed, Stanton and Childs got into a car and pulled away from the drugstore. Sandra had a shift, and since this wasn't her unit, she didn't stay behind. Slim Jim had stayed behind in the store in plainclothes, waiting for the signal from the manager that one of the men had arrived. Two uniforms were waiting in the break room with him.

"IAD's really got you by the balls, I hear," Childs said as he pulled onto the road and cut off another car.

"I don't think I'll be a cop much longer. After the lawsuit's done and they don't need me anymore, they'll force me to retire."

"You talked to your union rep yet?"

"No."

"Union should know about this shit. They hate that prick

Talano. I think they could really help you with this."

"I'm not sure I want to stick around."

His cell phone rang, and Stanton checked the ID. "Hey, Kyle, I'm busy right now, I'll call you—"

"I need help, Jon. Please." His voice sounded frantic, and he was sobbing.

"What's going on?"

"I'm hurt. I think I broke my leg. I'm fixing the fucking roof in the kitchen, and I fell and—"

"I'm calling 9-1-1 right now. What's your address?"

"No, no, I don't have insurance. I can't afford the ambulance, man. I need you to come get me. Please, Jon, my mom's not here. I don't have anyone but you. Please don't leave me, please."

"Okay, calm down, Kyle. What's your address?" Stanton wrote it down with a pen on the back of his hand. "Okay, I'll be there in ten minutes. All right?"

"All right."

Stanton hung up. "I need to make a quick stop."

"You shitting me?"

"Friend of mine broke his leg and can't afford an ambulance ride."

"Jon, you're fucking crazy, aren't you?"

"I can't leave him there, Danny. Just drop me off at his house. I'll check on him and then call an ambulance and pay for it myself."

Childs shook his head but grabbed Stanton's hand and looked at the address. He pressed the accelerator down and flipped on the red and blues attached as a box to the inside of the windshield. The siren wailing, he cut through two neighborhoods and took the express lane on the San Diego Freeway for nearly four miles before getting off and coming to a stop in front of an old home with a pointed roof.

"Shit looks rundown."

"He's renting. He's a young guy. I'll be right back."

Stanton got out and opened the gate of the chain-link fence. The old couch on the front porch looked as though it were infested with spiders, cobwebs on both sides. A few empty jars and tools were laid out, as well.

Stanton knocked then rang the doorbell. He tried the doorknob, and it turned. He opened the door and went inside.

The house was dark and cluttered. Stairs in front of him led up to the second floor, and a stairwell next to that led down into darkness. He went to the living room, but the house was so full of junk that he had to step over several piles and nearly lost his footing when he slipped on a plate lying on the floor.

"Kyle?" he shouted. He waited several moments, but no one answered.

Stanton hurried through the living room, noticing the old television with dials and rabbit-ear antennas. He passed a Victorian-era sofa with red-velvet upholstery and thought how out of place something so elegant looked there. He wondered if perhaps Kyle had some hoarding issues.

In the kitchen off to his left, water in a teapot boiled on an old gas stove. As he stepped into the kitchen and rounded the corner, the impact of the metal pipe crushed his nose and shattered one of his cheekbones. His mouth spewed blood, and he fell to his knees as the second blow connected with his neck. He flew onto his back, nearly unconscious. Another blow spattered his blood over the carpets and walls.

50

Stanton saw his mother sitting in the hospital bed, the cancer eating away at her. He remembered how lovely she had been. As time progressed, her hair fell out and her skin sagged, and she lost layer after layer of fat and muscle until she looked like a skeleton come to life. Toward the end, a single small nurse could lift her completely out of bed and place her in a wheelchair.

Light came back through the haze of memories, and he felt the floor against his back. One eye wouldn't open, and when he tried it, pain shot through his body. The other opened only slightly, and every object in his view was hazy and indistinct.

He could hear two voices. One was Kyle's. The other was male and older. Stanton couldn't place it, but it sounded so familiar. He tilted his head toward the voices, and the one he couldn't recognize stopped talking. Then footsteps left the room.

Kyle came and knelt over him. "Hey, Jon. How you feeling? Probably not too good, huh? I'll give you this: you took that beating like a champ. Honestly, I wanted it to kill you, and I thought for a second that I had. But you're still with us, huh?"

Stanton tried to open his mouth, but the pain in his jaw and teeth made him close it again. He needed to talk—to occupy Kyle, to convince him that he was his friend. Kyle would find it more difficult to cut up someone he saw as a friend.

"Real," Stanton gasped, his voice raspy and lisping because several teeth were missing, "name."

"Oh, my name? Don't you know? I bet you can guess. Go

ahead—guess."

Stanton stared at the ceiling. The pain overtook him as the shock wore off. Other than a warm sensation on his neck from the blood pouring out of a head wound, his body was numb, and he felt icy cold. His blood was rushing out of him too quickly. He would be dead soon. "Either," he rasped, "Calvin or Wes."

He chuckled. "Calvin at your service." Calvin looked at the door. "My dad says I shouldn't kill you. He thinks you came here with someone else, so he went out to check. Don't worry. If you did, he'll take care of them." Calvin reached down and searched him, pulling his firearm from the holster. "Whew, nice gun, man. It's pretty, all shiny. Do you use polish on it? I bet you use polish on it."

Stanton tried to move his arms and knew he could still control his right one. His legs felt detached from his body, and when he tried to move them, they wouldn't respond. His motor cortex had been damaged by a blow, and the entire left side of his body wouldn't move. He rolled to his stomach and tried to crawl, motivated only by fear and the pressing need to get away.

Calvin laughed. "How far do you think you can get?" He stood up and kicked Stanton's arm out from under him, causing his face to slap against the floor. He stomped on his head, making it bounce, and laughed again as the blood pooled around Stanton's face.

Calvin strolled to the counter, singing to himself, and opened a drawer. He pulled out a large kitchen knife and came back to Stanton. With his entire bodyweight, he slammed it into Stanton's leg.

Stanton screamed as the blade cut through flesh, deflected off his bone, and tore out the other side of his thigh. Calvin pulled it out and grabbed the back of Stanton's head, placing the blade against his throat.

"You know, Jon, I actually did like our time together on the beach. I like that you opened up to me about your wife and kids. I wouldn't worry about them, though. When I'm done with you, me and my daddy are makin' a little visit over there."

Stanton said one word, softly enough that he knew Calvin wouldn't hear.

Calvin leaned down. "What? Are you trying to beg for your life? 'Cause I'll listen. What did you say?"

"I said... *die*."

Stanton pulled out the revolver tucked into his waistband and fired two rounds into Calvin's chest. They went straight through him. Cotton from his shirt mixed with flesh, bone, and blood as the bullets ripped two gaping holes through his back.

Calvin collapsed on top of him, twitching and gurgling as he vomited blood. Stanton pulled the gun up with great effort and fired a single round into Calvin's throat. He stopped moving, and Stanton began to slowly roll him off as he heard footsteps outside in the hall.

Stanton crawled deeper into the kitchen, toward the oven, and pulled himself up to lean against it. He turned several knobs before the side door to the kitchen opened, and Ransom Talano stood there, shock running through his face as he saw the young man facedown on the linoleum.

Stanton attempted to raise the gun, but he was too slow. Ransom jumped on him and ripped it away. He fired a round into Stanton's stomach, and Stanton felt the air torn out of him.

Ransom went to Calvin and turned him over. His face was passive, revealing only the slightest glimpse of pain.

"He was my oldest. The one who was supposed to make something of himself. His mama is not gonna be happy about that." He held up the revolver and stepped close, aiming for Stanton's face.

Stanton tried to respond, but he could no longer breathe and was losing consciousness.

Ransom leaned down over him. "Good-bye, Detective."

Stanton held up the lighter that he had taken out of his pocket, and Ransom smiled at it before he noticed the hissing sound coming from his oven.

Stanton struck the lighter, igniting the gas that had been filling the room.

51

Doctor Searle finished the sutures on the young boy and stood back to evaluate his work. The eight-year-old boy had scraped his leg on some rough coral while surfing, and it'd taken a nasty chunk out of his flesh. But all in all, the leg was looking much better. With some antibiotics and rest, the boy would be back surfing in no time.

"Chris?" the nurse said, poking her head around the curtain.

"Uh-huh," Searle said as he ran his finger along the wound, testing the sutures.

"That detective is here to see you."

"I'll be right out."

He finished, tousled the boy's hair, and looked at his mother, who was sitting on a stool next to the bed. "He's gonna be fine. I'm prescribing some antibiotics and he should stay home from school tomorrow. Make sure he stays off that leg for a time."

All the worry in the woman's face melted away. "Thank you, Doctor."

"My pleasure." He opened the curtains and stepped through, closing them behind him.

In the hallway, a tall, slim man in a bad suit was standing with a buxom blonde.

"You Detective Porter?" Dr. Searle asked.

"Yes," the female said.

"Like I told you on the phone, they're stable and doing fine. The big guy, Childs—he's a tough son of a bitch. That blow he took to the left parietal bone would've shot me straight to hell, but he's hanging in there. The other detective… ah…"

"Jon Stanton," Sandra said.

"Right. He's in stable condition, but he's burned fairly badly. Second- and third-degree burns over at least twenty percent of his body. We're going to have to watch him, but he's young and strong. I've seen weaker men make it out with worse just fine. The round in his stomach went clean through and thankfully didn't hit his spine. We'll have to keep a close eye on it, but he's extremely lucky."

"What about the other two?" the male detective asked.

"The young male was dead from several gunshot wounds before he ever got here. The other body we found survived for a few hours but died of smoke inhalation. What the hell happened at that house anyway?"

Sandra felt a knot the size of a softball in her stomach. On the way over, she'd been biting her nails, something she hadn't done since she was thirteen years old.

She turned and looked down the hall toward the ICU, where Stanton recovered in a plastic isolation unit. She rushed over to his room, and the door had a glass window. Stanton lay in a bed, propped up by several pillows. His eyes were closed. *Young and strong, that's what the doctor had said. Young and strong.*

After a few seconds, she saw the slightest trace of movement. His eyes partially opened, and a faint grin came to his lips before his eyes closed again.

PSIA information can be obtained
www.ICGtesting.com
ed in the USA
100350280622
LV00005B/117